Just Jake

A novel

Erik P. Block

Copyright © 2011 by Erik P. Block.

Library of Congress Control Number:		2011909103
ISBN:	Hardcover	978-1-4628-8278-6
	Softcover	978-1-4628-8277-9
	Ebook	978-1-4628-8279-3

All rights reserved. No part of this book may be reproduced or transmitted in any form or by any means, electronic or mechanical, including photocopying, recording, or by any information storage and retrieval system, without permission in writing from the copyright owner.

This is a work of fiction. Names, characters, places and incidents either are the product of the author's imagination or are used fictitiously, and any resemblance to any actual persons, living or dead, events, or locales is entirely coincidental.

This book was printed in the United States of America.

To order additional copies of this book, contact:
Xlibris Corporation
1-888-795-4274
www.Xlibris.com
Orders@Xlibris.com
100330

Just Jake

This book is dedicated to my family, my friends,
my teachers—everyone who helped me create the
memories and feelings that became Jake's story.
Some of you will undoubtedly see exactly
where your influence exists in this book,
and some of you won't.

But believe me: you're all here.

Chapter 1

I'm halfway through my shift at the gas station, daydreaming about the moment I'll finally get off work tonight, when this girl walks in with two other girls trailing her. That's how it strikes me. Not three girls walking in together. One girl and two sidekicks.

The first girl is average height—maybe about 5'6" or so—with blonde hair that flows down her shoulders in thick, loose curls. She's wearing a yellow sundress that is one size too small and a yellow and red plaid golf hat, cocked lazily over one eye. She's solidly built. Definitely not fat, but not skinny either. She has one of those faces that makes it difficult to tell whether or not she's wearing make-up. She's not pretty exactly, but something about her makes it hard to look away. Her eyes are deep brown and seem to take up her whole face. Below each eye is a random dousing of freckles; above each is a well-groomed thin arc of an eyebrow. Her nose is small and roundish and makes me think of a rabbit. *She probably reads decent books* is my first thought. *Probably claims to like "all kinds of music"* is my second.

The other two girls look like a comedic duo. One is tall and thin with long brown hair as straight as a pin and freckles on her face and shoulders. Her legs are long and frail and her arms move like wind-blown tree branches when she walks. As if her body wasn't enough to force the inevitable stork or ostrich comparison, she has the misfortune of having been born with a notably bird-like face as well. The other girl is really short and chubby enough to look bad in a halter-top but not quite chubby enough to know it. In green flip-flops, her feet look too small for her body. She walks like a penguin, her body loping pendulously back and forth with each step. She could topple over at any moment.

I watch them giggle their way to the back of the store and spend what seems like too long in front of the soda coolers. They laugh and whisper and lean into each other the way girls do and I keep wondering when Chubby is going to fall over. They're making their way to the front of the store so I give myself a quick once-over. Size 13 Converse All Stars, khaki carpenter pants that aren't quite long enough to cover up my mismatched socks, and an untucked red and blue polo shirt that hangs off me like a tent tied to a flagpole. I'm not exactly the suavest guy in the world anyway, but this isn't how I would prefer to be dressed in this situation. They step to the counter and I try to act bored and uninterested while they pay for their drinks. The tall one gets a glass-bottled root beer, the chubby one a diet something. Yellow Girl gets lemonade in a can, which I didn't even know we had.

"Hi, Jacob," says Yellow Girl. I'm caught off guard. Why does she know my name? I'm brainstorming possibilities when she points out that it plainly says "Jacob" on my nametag. Duh. She's heading for the door and I need to speak to her, need to say something.

"Just Jake," I say.

"What was that?" she asks.

"Just Jake," I stupidly repeat.

"Well, you have a swell day, Just Jake," she says. She turns to walk out and as the door closes, one blonde curl is wisped to the side, revealing a small, red question mark tattooed behind her ear. She disappears from view and I feel weird and floaty, kind of like when you put your shoes back on after roller-skating.

My name is Jacob Withers. People usually just call me Jake. I'm sixteen years old. I'll be a junior in a few weeks, but for now I'm working just short of full time at a QuikMart a ways down the street from my high school. The job pretty much sucks. I mean, I'm sure there are worse jobs out there, but mine is pretty frickin' boring. In a nutshell, here's an average day at my job: *Shuffle shuffle grab shuffle shuffle cha-ching shuffle shuffle bye repeat.* Donuts and coffee in the morning, sodas and candy bars during the day, drunk munchies at night, and gas, smokes and nudie books everywhere in between. Pretty much mindless. And to top it off, the boss' shitty old crackle box is eternally tuned to conservative talk radio.

I usually manage to tune out the zombie voices as I work through my day, but today I heard something that I can't get out of my head: The average life span for a human being has reached 78 years. It suddenly occurs to me that, assuming I am average (and I am—at best), I have lived, for better or worse, less than 25 percent of my life. Two more years of high school, four or five years of college if I decide to go that route, forty or fifty years of working, a couple years of watching TV with a blanket on my lap, and then I go to sleep and never wake up. And that's if I'm lucky. I'll be dodging cancer, STDs and car accidents the whole way. And what have I done so far? If I break my life down into a list of chronological accomplishments worthy of noting, it looks something like this: learned to talk, learned to walk, learned to play the piano, learned to piss in a toilet, made it through grade school, currently fighting to maintain at least a portion of my sanity during the adolescent years, which are, of course, pass or fail. We've yet to determine whether that will make my list of achievements.

Midnight finally rolls around, and I close up the store and head home. I'm walking around to the back parking lot when I hear someone yell out my name. I whirl and scan the parking lot. It's dark and I don't see anyone, so I turn and head for my car again when I hear a giggle in the shadows on the wall of the store. I can't see much, but I can make out the outline of a body squatted down on the pavement, leaning against the wall. I smell cigarette smoke.

"Hey, Jaker." A girl's voice, much closer now.

Jaker? What the hell is that all about? "Do I know you?"

The shape stands up straight and comes out of the shadow. It's Yellow Girl. She's still wearing the same dress. She's holding the plaid hat in her right hand, and smoking a cigarette with her left. The night is thick and sticky and her dress clings to her in spots. Her hair is flat on top from the hat, and flows out in every direction, falling over her shoulders, over her collarbones, down her back. Her eyes look dark and sunken.

I realize suddenly that she is beautiful. Right here in this moment, in this heat, half of her body in shadow, the other half illuminated by the flickering light of a street lamp, she is so beautiful it aches. I want to touch her, but I don't even know her name.

Something's obviously wrong. I should say something to her—try to make her feel better.

"What are you doing here?" *Nice one.*

"Oh, not much," she replies and kicks a pebble across the parking lot. "Waiting for a knight to rescue me. Or a fireman. Or pirate. Somebody."

"Is there anything I can help you with?" I wanted to say something 'nice,' but it came out all wrong.

"I doubt that, Jaker. I doubt that very much." Truth be told, I kind of like the 'Jaker' thing, but I don't know where it came from or what it means. So I ask her.

"Why do we do any number of the things we do, Jaker?" she answers. "Do you ever ask yourself that? I bet you do. You seem like you do. What am I doing here, Jake? I mean, really? I don't know. Something told me to come here. I know that sounds dumb, and I don't know if you believe in stuff like that. I sure as hell don't. But I'm here. And so are you." Her words come out in quick little bursts, like she doesn't have time to think. Maybe she doesn't need to.

Retreating into the shadow, she lets her body slump back to the ground, pulls a pack of cigarettes from her purse, takes one out and lights it. She lets the first drag hang in her lungs, really savors it, then opens her mouth and lets the smoke roll out slowly, curling over her lip and disappearing into the air overhead. Her lips form an "O" and she whistles a long, high note as she pushes the rest of the smoke out of her lungs and into the night. She giggles again, crosses her legs, and pats the pavement next to her. I sit.

"Do you smoke, Jaker? I'd've offered you one, but I didn't take you for a smoker."

"No, I don't. Thanks, though." Wonder why she pegged me a nonsmoker? Am I not "cool" enough? I know I'm not exactly James Dean, especially in my work get-up, but when I'm not at work I have a look that works okay. And I've always *wanted* a black biker jacket. That's got to count for something.

"Not cigarettes, anyway, huh, Jaker? Don't lie to me." She elbows my ribs playfully—she probably does that to everyone.

"Yeah, that's right," I say. "Not cigarettes, anyway." She bends one leg, pulling it to her chest, and her dress rides up high on her thighs. I'm glad it's dark so she can't see me looking.

"So, Jake?"

"Yeah?"

"So, so, so." She looks away and folds her hands together in front of her. "What now?"

"You still haven't told me why you're here. Not really, anyway," I say. "You been crying?" I immediately wish I could suck the words back into my mouth.

"So I have, Jaker. So I have," she says. "It's just, well, something I do. A lot."

"Any of my business?" I ask, surprised by the relatively smooth demeanor I'm managing to maintain, considering my normal reactions to the presence of girls—especially girls in tight sundresses who smoke cigarettes with the cool indifference of a '50s pin-up model.

"Well, probably not, considering I just met you. But maybe. Care to know?"

"Sure."

"I feel kind of stupid about it. You'll laugh." She looks away again.

"I won't laugh. Honest. Swear to God."

"It's my birthday. I'm eighteen." She tips her chin back and forces a long chain of smoke out between her pursed lips and into the air above her, where it dissipates into the darkness.

"So? That's good, right? You can buy smokes. And lottery tickets. And you can vote, too, if you want," I say. It isn't exactly the same as saying *Hi, I'm a big tool*, but it has exactly the same effect.

"Yeah. Vote. *Woo hoo.*" She drags on her cigarette, then pulls it from her lips and studies it. She turns to me and our eyes meet. "You ever watch the Discovery Channel? Animal Planet? Anything like that?"

"Yeah," I answer. "A lot, actually. Why?"

"Ever seen anything about seahorses?"

"I'm not sure," I answer, sifting through the random wildlife knowledge in my brain: penguins, gorillas, hyenas, blue whales . . . nope, no seahorses. "I don't think so."

"Seahorses are pretty amazing, Jake. And you know why? Do you know how seahorses reproduce? How their babies are born?"

"No, guess I don't."

"The father gives birth to them. Honest. The mother plants her eggs in this pouch on the father. And then, after the eggs hatch, the father shoots all the little seahorses out of his pouch. He actually *gives birth* to them. Isn't that wild?"

"Yeah," I say. "I guess it is. What does this have to do with your birthday?"

"Nothing." She looks confused.

"You were going to tell me why you were crying, remember? You mentioned that it was your birthday and then you started talking about seahorses. I'm not seeing the connection."

"The connection is this, Jake." Her brow furrows and her nose pulls upward. She sighs. "Seahorse fathers carry their babies in a pouch until they are born, and mine can't even . . . nevermind."

"Can't even what? Did your dad forget your birthday or something?"

"No. Of course he didn't *forget*. What kind of dad would *forget* his daughter's birthday? He just . . ."

"He just *what?*"

"I told you; you're going to laugh."

"I won't laugh."

"He didn't get me what I wanted."

"*That's* what you're crying about?"

"I knew you'd laugh."

"I'm not laughing. Who's laughing?"

The wind picks up and she looks away again, rubs her legs with her hands.

"So, what was it? I mean, what was it that you wanted?" I ask.

"A car."

"A car?" I ask, more than a little confused.

"Yeah. A car. I mean, I already have a car, obviously. I wanted a *different* car."

"A car for your birthday?" I ask. "Isn't that kind of . . . I don't know . . . expensive?"

"Not for my dad," she says. "He owns a bank."

"He owns a bank? Weird. I guess I never really thought of banks as being owned by anyone."

"Well, they are. And my dad owns one. A few, actually. It's a chain."

"Like McDonald's?"

"I don't know. Sort of, I guess."

"Well, what did he get you instead?"

"He put some money into some sort of account to help me pay for college."

"Sounds alright to me," I say. "How much money?"

"A few thousand," she says. "Five or six, I think."

"Damn. I got a bike for my birthday. I think it was used." She's not looking at me and I'm pretty sure she's not listening. "How come I haven't seen you around before?" I ask. "Do you live in Browerton?"

"Nope," she says, then stands suddenly and wipes gravel off the back of her dress. "Well, Jaker, I better get going. Since I'm not really sure what I came here for, I really have no way of knowing when to leave, right?"

"I guess," I say, wishing I knew what to say to make her stay.

"So now would be as good a time as any?" She tilts her head and shrugs; the strap of her dress brushes her earlobe.

"I s'pose," I answer. "Do you need a ride or anything?"

"I have a car, remember?" And with that she turns, and I watch the yellow fabric of her dress tightly hug her hips and thighs as she walks along the store's wall and disappears around the corner. I still don't know her name.

Chapter 2

If I work the morning shift, I get done in time to go fishing at the dam or skateboarding in the bank parking lot or else sometimes I just sit at home in the air conditioning and smoke pot in the basement. If I work the late shift, like I did tonight, I'm out of there by a little after midnight, lighting up a bowl in my maroon Ford Pinto by 12:20 and home a little after 12:30 to get wasted alone and watch infomercials.

Tonight I pull into the driveway a little later than usual, my head buzzing with images of Yellow Girl: a wisp of smoke escaping her plump lips, the soft curve of her thighs, her fingers drumming the pavement next to her. I can feel my head thickening from the bowl I've just smoked as I make my way down the stairs to the den, where I waste no time packing a second one. Clicking the T.V. on, I pat the couch cushion next to me, inviting an absent Yellow Girl to have a seat, cuddle up and stay awhile. On the screen, a muscle bound, pony-tailed man attacks a fragile-looking piece of exercise equipment with ferocious intensity, grinning like a fucking idiot all the while. My thoughts still lingering on tonight's encounter, I head upstairs to check the fridge for beers. I find three cans of Miller Lite hiding in the crisper, grab them, and head back downstairs. Popping the tab from one can, I tip my head back and guzzle until it's half gone. The buzzing in my head intensifies and I lean back and sink into the soft cushions of the old, flowered couch and watch the room spin. I imagine Yellow Girl's head on my shoulder, her thick blonde curls tickling my neck. My hand moves slowly down her smooth thigh, over and over, like petting a cat.

An hour or two later, I'm snapped out of my substance-induced pseudo-coma by the sound of footsteps coming down the stairs. The T.V. screen is silent and snowy, the station having gone off the air. The door at the bottom of the stairwell flies open and my mother trips into the room like a stage actress botching her entrance. A cartoon bear with half-closed eyes smiles at me from her nightshirt, and pleads, "Please

13

don't wake me 'til spring." Mumbling to herself, she pulls a stool to the center of the room, climbs onto it, and begins unscrewing the bulb from the light fixture. She removes the bulb, passes it under her nose several times, shakes it next to her ear, then throws it into the chair in the corner of the room. Next, she goes for the lamp on the end table—the only light in the room that's on. Before I have time to realize what she's doing and stop her, she grips the searing hot bulb and her skin sizzles as she twists it out of the fixture. Oblivious to the pain, she tosses this bulb onto the chair as well, where it strikes the other bulb with a hollow *tink.*

She stands, lopsided, in the center of the room, her arms dangling limply at her sides, hands fidgeting nervously, eyes hollow and lifeless as a skull. Her lips open and close rhythmically, a silent incantation, and her body sways from side to side.

I've been around long enough to know what's going on, even in my state. Mom's having one of her "episodes." She's bipolar and goes through these phases where she becomes, more or less, someone else. I've never really seen it much myself, but Dad has told me about it. He said there were times years ago when she got so bad she didn't even know who he was. She wouldn't even recognize her own house or her own husband or anything—she would think she was kidnapped or something and he was holding her hostage. Weird shit like that. The way Dad explains it, I picture her like something out of a horror movie: cowered in the corner, her hair sticking out in every direction like the bride of Frankenstein, her skin damp and greenish. Of course, he only talks about that stuff when he's really drunk. More on that later.

Her doctor says her condition would be manageable, but she refuses to keep up on her medication. She probably won't remember tonight when she comes out of this, but she'll likely have a reminder in the form of tender, burned fingertips. She doesn't resist when I take her by the arm and lead her to the bathroom to run cold water on her hands. She does resist a little when I shake five Tylenol P.M.s out of the bottle and feed them to her one by one, then take her back to bed, where I practically have to hold her down until the drugs kick in and she starts snoring. If I don't drug her, she'll bounce off the walls, smoking cigarettes and chewing her fingernails, until I go insane too, which I don't intend to do. Not today, anyway.

I take it upon myself to call the hospital where she volunteers during the summer and let them know that she won't be in today. She only volunteers there a couple days a week now, but she used to work there full time. Over 20 years without a single moment of recognition outside of a few free tee shirts and an annual Thank You Banquet, yet she continues to treat the job like it's the American presidency. She won't miss a day with her "other family" (that's what she calls the patients) for anything short of debilitating illness which, in the worst times, her bipolar disorder is. Personally, I think she just can't stand spending too much time with her real family. If she's not volunteering, she's usually at some class or other—yoga, pilates, tai chi, you name it. And if it's not a class, it's a city council meeting or a church function or something with my brother, Kyle. He's ten and has cerebral palsy. Her shrink says she has to keep busy to keep herself occupied and feeling important or whatever. For now, all she needs to do is stay in her room and sleep.

Five pills will probably be enough to keep Mom out until at least mid afternoon, so I have to be up early to get Kyle up and feed him his breakfast. It's after 4:30 a.m. now and Mom usually gets Kyle up by 8:00 at the latest. I set my alarm for 9:30 and crawl into bed, hoping to dream of the girl in the yellow dress.

The alarm clock's buzzer goes off and, fumbling to hit the snooze bar, I knock it to the floor. I was dreaming, but not about Yellow Girl. It was one of those dreams that started with me getting out of bed, so I had no idea that I was dreaming. I went upstairs to get Kyle up, but he wasn't in his room. His bed was perfectly made (which it never is) like he'd never even been there. I ran into my mom's room but she wasn't there either. I found Kyle's wheelchair in the kitchen, tipped on its side. One of the wheels was still spinning. Then I heard a wet, gurgling sound coming from the living room, where I found Kyle on the floor, stomach down, dragging himself across the carpet by his elbows like a private at basic training. His eyes were wide awake and alert. He looked up at me and I knew that he could actually *see* me. He opened his mouth, and a thin string of white spit pulled between his lips, then broke. *Kkkk-cchhh,* he said. *Cchhhh-fffff. He's trying to talk,* I thought. *Kyle's trying to say something.* Slowly and painfully, he dragged himself across the thick shag carpet. I could see his raw, pink elbows spotted with droplets of blood like pinholes. *Ffffssssss . . .* he said. His mouth opened and closed like a fish on a dock, gasping for air. I tried to get closer to Kyle, but my dream body wouldn't let me. He crawled closer and closer, but I felt myself floating further away. *Jjjj-jjjaa,* he said, just as the sound of the alarm pulled me back to the surface.

I jump out of bed and take the stairs three at a time on my way up to Kyle's room. His bedroom door is open, as always, and he's tucked securely in his bed. His wheelchair sits a few feet from his bedside. Mom forgot to put the side rail on the bed up, which is fine, 'cause I can never get the damn thing to unlock anyway.

"Kyle," I say. "Time to get up, dude." I shake his shoulder a little and first one eye opens, then the other. I pull his blanket back and see that he's wearing a pair of red sweatpants and one of his many horse t-shirts. Mom must have already been too gone to change him into his pajamas before she put him to bed. I cup one hand under his neck to sit him up and find that he left a sloppy, wet surprise for the back of my hand in the form of a pool of fresh drool. You'd think I'd be used to stuff like that by now, and I guess I am, sort of, but I still hate it. I guess drool's not as bad as changing diapers, which is also on the long list of joyful activities I encounter in an average day of taking care of my brother, the wonderboy. I hold him upright by the back of his neck with one hand and, one at a time, swing his legs over the side of the bed. A clicking sound issues from the back of Kyle's throat. Some kind of reflex or something, I guess.

"I had a dream about you last night," I say. "You got out of your chair somehow and you were trying to talk to me." I slide his chair closer to the bed and slip one arm under his legs and the other around his lower back. "All right, we're going to the chair, Buddy. On three," I say. "One, two, three," and I hoist him off the bed and into his chair. At least he didn't have a seizure this time. I swear to God the kid gets a kick out of waiting until I pick him up to start flopping. He has at least a couple seizures a day that I know of. Maybe more.

In the kitchen, I grab the plastic tray that attaches to Kyle's chair and snap it into place. There's only one box of cereal in the cupboard, which makes my choice a little easier. Not that Kyle knows what he's eating anyway. I pour a few flakes into a bowl and drink some milk straight from the carton before pouring the rest of it over Kyle's cereal. I've found that it helps to let the cereal get soggy before trying to feed it to him because he has trouble swallowing. Feeding Kyle is sort of like pouring liquid down a clogged drain. You just sort of dump a little in and wait for it to go down before you dump any more. He gurgles and chokes and drools and spits up and you just keep feeding until it's gone.

Once we've got the whole bowl of cereal down, I try to pour some of the milk from the bowl into his mouth. He coughs and sputters and most of it ends up on his bib, so I just dump the rest down the drain and push him into the living room. I turn on the T.V. and flip through the channels, hoping to find an old rerun of Mr. Ed, Kyle's favorite show. I find a show on Animal Planet about a barnyard veterinarian, and I figure there's as good a chance that it'll show horses as anything else I'll find. Kyle *loves* horses. He's never seen one in real life, but he always wiggles his shoulders and laughs his deep, throaty laugh when he sees one on T.V. or in a book. I've always wanted to bring him to a farm or somewhere where he could see a real horse. Maybe even sit on one. But since I don't know anyone who owns a horse, I'd kind of like to buy one someday if I ever have enough money. Maybe get a little farm out in the middle of nowhere and have Kyle move in with me.

For now, though, the best I can do is leave him in front of the T.V. staring at the images of two Appaloosas galloping across a grassy pasture, their shiny manes flowing behind them.

Since the day Kyle was born, I have been like a shadow in my house. Don't get me wrong—I know Kyle needs lots of attention, but my mom sometimes barely seems to notice that I'm in the room. On the bright side, this allows me to do pretty much whatever I want, whenever I want. What more could a sixteen year old ask for, right? But I don't really know my mom; I mean, who she really is. I know things can't be too easy for her, with her illness and taking care of Kyle and trying to make sense of her more-or-less nonexistent marriage. She just doesn't have a lot of time to devote to me, which is fine, 'cause I'm sixteen. I can take care of myself.

I was only six when Kyle was born, but I remember pretty well what it was like before him. She was pretty much the perfect mom. My memories of her remind me of the mothers on the late-night reruns of *Donna Reed* and *Leave it to Beaver* that I sometimes catch on *Nick at Nite* after work. Not that I necessarily believe the memories. Memory can be a slippery thing; even at my age, I know that. But she was a good mom, anyway.

Mostly, I remember my sixth birthday party. I came upstairs as soon as I woke up and Mom was sitting at the table. In front of my spot was a bowl of *Crunch Berries*—my favorite cereal.

"Happy birthday!" she said as I sat down to eat. "Hope you like your present."

"What present?" I asked, shoveling pink berries into my mouth.

"Your favorite cereal," Mom joked. "That's all I got you for your birthday this year. There's a whole box; you can have more when you're done with that bowl."

"That's not all you got me, Mom!" I said, my mouth so full of cereal that it's a wonder she understood me.

"'Fraid so, honey," she said. "Your dad and I were going to get you socks and underwear, but we thought you'd like this better." Even as young as I was, I knew she was up to something. I finished my bowl of cereal and handed the bowl to my mom to get me more.

"You're a big boy, now," she said. "You can get your own." She took the box from the kitchen counter, set it down on the table in front of me, and sat down. I stood on my chair, tongue poking out the side of my mouth in intense concentration, and struggled with the box top, then the cellophane inside. Inside the box, the corner of a small piece of paper poked up out of the colorful cereal. I dug my hand in and pulled it out. Written on the paper in green marker was a few short lines of verse that I read out loud (I had more or less learned how to read by the time I was four). I don't remember exactly what they said, but they constituted a clue that led me to another sheet of paper with another clue and so on. After running around the house, garage, and backyard, feverishly searching for the next piece of the puzzle while my mother watched, smiling, I finally reached the end of the hunt. The last clue led me into my bedroom where I found under my bed a large box wrapped in brightly-colored paper. I tore into the gift like a lion ripping meat from a carcass, and under all that paper I found the most wondrous thing my six-year-old eyes had ever seen. Castle Greyskull, fortress of the mighty He-Man, was actually in my hands, and it was all mine. Its hollow eyes stared back at me from above its fanged, drawbridge mouth. It was the only thing I'd wanted for my birthday, and the only thing I'd asked for. I'd talked about it for months, and now here it was. I tore the box to pieces, pulled the green castle out, and splayed it before me.

"This is so awesome, Mom," I said. "Thanks."

"There's more, Jake," she said. "Look in the bottom of the box." She pushed the box across the floor to me and I could see a small white envelope inside. I opened the envelope and pulled out a Garfield birthday card. Written inside—again in green marker—were several more lines of verse. I looked at Mom, my face scrunched questioningly.

"Another clue?" I asked.

"Another clue," she said. "Well, what does it say?" Again, I read the lines out loud and they seemed to suggest the garage. "The garage?" I asked. "I was already in there."

"Well, we better go look again," she said, "if that's what the clue says." We walked out to the garage, cluttered with tools, scrap wood, and oily old rags. I scanned the wooden walls for another clue, a brightly-colored gift, something. Then in the very back corner, next to an old wooden ladder, I saw a large rectangular shape shrouded by a blue tarp.

I turned to my mother and opened my mouth to ask her what it was, when she said, "Go ahead, Jake. Pull the tarp off. See what's underneath." I ran to the shrouded object and yanked the tarp to the side. Underneath was an upright piano. The wood was dull and scratched, the keys chipped in spots, but it was the most amazing thing I had ever seen.

"Is this mine, Mom?" I asked, rubbing my hands together excitedly. "Is this for me?"

"Of course it is, silly," she answered. "It is your birthday, isn't it?"

I had started messing around with my mom's old miniature chord organ when I was 3 years old. I was able to play things like *Mary Had a Little Lamb* and *Twinkle, Twinkle* by ear within a few weeks, and I had learned most of Bach's *Toccata and Fugue in D Minor* and all of Beethoven's *Moonlight Sonata* before my fifth birthday. Of course I had always wanted a piano, but even at the age of five, I instinctually understood that my family could not afford one. It had never occurred to me to even ask, and yet, right here before me was my very own piano. I reached out with my right hand and played a C Minor chord. Both the E sharp and the G were slightly out of tune, but I didn't care. My left hand joined my right on the keyboard and together they sailed through a series of scales and transitioned into the beginning of *The William Tell Overture.*

I looked up at my mother and smiled, only to see her beginning to cry. She brought her hand to her face and covered her mouth and nose, squinting her damp eyes. She wrapped both arms around me, resting her chin on the top of my head and we swayed together as I played.

Most of the memories of Mom that I have from my early childhood were like this one: happy and carefree. A few years after Kyle was born, everything started to change. I remember one day—I must have been around 8 or 9—that we were going to go to the zoo together. My grandma came over and picked up Kyle for the day, and it was going to be just Dad, Mom, and me. I was up super early 'cause I'd been excited for weeks and I went into my parents' bedroom to see if we could go yet. Their bedroom door was open just a crack and I could see that a light was on, so I swung the door the rest of the way open. Mom was in bed, facing the wall, and I could hear that she was sobbing quietly. Dad was in his underwear, standing in front of the mirror. He just stood there with both hands planted on the top of the dresser like they were the only thing holding him up. He was whispering something but I couldn't make out the words. I was certain that he could see me in the mirror, standing behind him, but his eyes never moved. He just looked into his own eyes, his brow furrowed like he was asking himself a question he couldn't answer. Despite my excitement for our trip to the zoo, I knew even then that something was very wrong, and I closed the door and went back to my bedroom. I lay in bed with the covers pulled over my face and cried for what felt like a very long time. I didn't see Mom for the rest of the day, but I knew that she was in her room, probably crying with the covers over her face like I was. Usually I push that memory as far back in my mind as I can get it. It's sort of like the beginning of the end. That sounds dumb, I know, but it's true.

After I get a little breakfast for myself, I lie down on the couch in the living room. Kyle is breathing loudly and I can't tell if he's sleeping or not. Flipping through the channels, I find a documentary about ocean life. Little fluorescent-colored fish dart in and out between the fuzzy arms of a coral reef while a huge, black-eyed eel slithers through the water hunting them, its teeth bared. One tiny fish, light blue with a pink stripe running the length of its body, pops out of a nook in the coral and directly into the path of the eel, which plunges ahead with one swish of its muscular body, scooping the fish into its jaws. The screen switches to a car commercial and I roll over and face the back of the couch. I close my eyes and match my breathing to Kyle's until I feel myself drifting into sleep.

I dream about my father—the day six years ago when he lost his job. I come upstairs to get ready for school. It's picture day, so I'm wearing a blue and yellow striped polo shirt that Mom gave me. For some reason, the dream version of the shirt doesn't have sleeves (the real version smelled like a wet basement but was, otherwise, intact). Usually when I come upstairs in the morning Dad is sitting at the table dressed up for work with the newspaper and a cup of coffee. He'll say good morning and sometimes fix me something to eat before dropping me off at school on his way to work. Today, though, the kitchen is empty, quiet except for the *tick tick* of the old handmade wall clock Mom bought at the church bazaar.

I stand on my tiptoes to get a cup from the cupboard and pour myself a glass of orange juice. It's almost time to leave for school, so I check to see if Dad's in the bathroom, but it's empty. I walk to Mom and Dad's room at the end of hall and open the door slowly. I see the back of Mom's head, her messy hair spilling out over the top of the comforter. No sign of Dad. I shake Mom's shoulder a little and she wakes up for just a second, locks her dead eyes with mine, then lays her head back down.

"Mom," I say. "Where's Dad?"

She doesn't reply.

"Mom," I say again. "Dad's not here. I need a ride to school." I shake her shoulder again but she doesn't stir. Unsure what to do, I head out to the living room and take a seat on the couch. I turn on the T.V. just as Dad comes through the front door, hair mussed up, shirt half-buttoned, eyes as lifeless as Mom's. He's wearing the same clothes he was wearing when he left the house after supper the night before. He stumbles into the room and I can smell the booze on him, mixed with something else. Campfire, maybe? In the dream, Dad has a big beard and long, curly hair. He sits down on the couch and looks at me without saying a word.

"I need a ride to school, Dad," I say. "We gotta hurry up." Then, as dreams often will, it starts to get weird. Dad picks me up and carries me outside, and suddenly we're at my school. My teacher, Miss Fazen, is at the front of the room lecturing, when my dad grabs her in his arms and kisses her. His hand moves up her leg and disappears beneath her flowered dress. Miss Fazen's hands are on Dad's chest, trying to push him away, but he holds her tightly and keeps kissing, keeps moving his hand back and forth under her dress. He turns Miss Fazen's body so her back is to the class and both of his hands are under her dress now, caressing her legs and butt. His eyes pop open and he's staring directly at me. My eyes lock with his and I can't look away. *What about Mom?* I try to scream, but my voice won't work—nothing leaves my mouth but a rasping breath. *What about Mom? She loves you!* Miss Fazen is pounding on Dad's chest now and screaming, the sound muffled by his gaping mouth, and I wake up.

I don't know where the end of the dream came from, but most of it was pretty close to what really happened. My dad was fired that day, and hasn't held a job since. This is because he is, to put it simply, a drunk. He is a worthless loser and why my mom is still married to him belongs right up there with whether God is real and the whereabouts of Jimmy Hoffa on the list of life's great mysteries. It's actually not that big of a deal most of the time. He isn't here that often. He comes and goes. I know he drinks and plays darts, and other than that, I have no idea where my father is or what he is doing most of the time.

My mom's dad died a few years back and left my mom a bunch of money, which she stupidly keeps in an account that she shares with my dad. Ever since that day, my dad has disappeared for days at a time, occasionally coming home drunk and passing out in my mom's bed, only to get up, start drinking, and stumble out the door again until the next time he decides to grace us with his presence. Not that he didn't drink and disappear before Grandpa died, he is just able to do it all the time now, which is probably better for us. And as for him, I really don't give a shit.

The upside of having a fucked-up dad is that I can steal his booze and pot without him ever knowing. He keeps a pretty good stock of vodka, spiced rum, and scotch in one of the kitchen counters, and there's usually at least a little weed in one of several hiding spots, even when he hasn't been around for a while. The downside is that I'm smart enough to realize that I'm pretty much headed down his road. I don't know if that makes me want to laugh or cry.

Chapter 3

I don't see Mom again until the next morning when I come upstairs for breakfast. Obviously back in the land of the living, she's seated at the kitchen table, feeding oatmeal to Kyle. She looks up at me for a second, but can't quite manage a "hello" or "good morning" or "oh, that's right—I have two sons." She's too busy with her "let's all spoil Kyle" baby talk. What transpires is a typical scene of my mom with Kyle, complete with my not-quite-verbal, eye-rolling comments:

"My little man likes his oatmeal, doesn't he?"

Good god. Is she serious?

"We dribbled a little on our napkin, didn't we, Kylie?"

He's retarded, mom. He does this every day. Quit acting like spilling food is the fucking moon landing.

"Mommy is SO proud of her little man."

He's ten, mom. He's not a baby. And just what are you so proud of? The fact that he is so gracious as to let you spoon feed him?

And now, should we see what happens when ol' Jake tries to get a word in with his dear mother?

"Hey, ma."

Nothing.

"MOM . . ."

Nope.

"Mom, I'm going to skip work today, take a small group of hostages at the mall, and punctuate the ensuing standoff by offing myself in front of a crowd of hundreds."

If this were a movie, she would respond with something like "That's nice, dear," indicating that she had heard me, but not listened. Here's the response she opts for instead:

" . . ."

Typical.

Just Jake | 23

My shift at the QuikMart passes without incident. I spend most of the day daydreaming about Yellow Girl. My heart pounds in my chest every time the bell on the door dings, and I stop whatever I'm doing and look to see if it's her walking in, which it never is.

When I get home from work there's a note on the table from my mom. It says "Took Kyle to clinic. Not feeling well—Mom." I pull some thawed hamburger from the fridge, form a couple of bloody, pink patties and throw them in a pan. The clock above the stove says 4:33. We don't have any buns so I throw the meat onto some bread and sit down to eat. I wish I had a beer but there are none in the fridge.

Jeopardy comes on at five, so I lay down on the couch to watch, and the next thing I know, I'm waking up to the phone ringing. It's dark now and I stumble to the phone and pick it up.

"Hello?"

"Jake? Hi, it's Mom."

"Yeah?"

"Did Helen show up yet?"

"No," I say. Helen does in-home care for my brother when my mom and I aren't around. "I don't think she comes today."

"Oh?" she says. "I thought she did. Anyway, her number's on the list there by the phone. I thought I had it in my purse but I can't find it. Could you call her and let her know that she doesn't need to come today? The doctor thinks Kyle might have some kind of pneumonia again so they're going to do some tests and keep him overnight."

"How 'bout I just give you the number and you call her?" I say. I read the number off to her.

"All right," she says.

"Yeah," I say, and I hang up.

My brother gets pneumonia and spends a few nights in the hospital at least once a year. He has trouble swallowing because of his cerebral palsy, so it's easy for him to end up inhaling bacteria into his lungs and getting an infection. Mom told me all about it when I was pretty young and, sure enough, Kyle has managed to have pneumonia off and on ever since. It's really no big deal, though. Pretty much the same routine every time. Kyle doesn't feel well and coughs a lot, Mom brings him into the hospital, they give him medicine for a couple days and he comes home.

I consider heading next door to smoke some weed with my neighbor, Al—probably the closest thing I have to a friend—but it's already kind of late and I work the early shift tomorrow. I go down the stairs to my room, set an alarm for 7:15 a.m. and crawl into bed.

I wake up from a dream at 5:04 am. Me and Yellow Girl were underwater, swimming around a giant staircase. She was wearing the yellow dress and plaid hat. Shadows of giant birds kept appearing on the staircase, but when I looked up, there was nothing there. I want to go back to sleep and try to finish the dream, but I'm thirsty and I have to pee. Eyes still stinging with sleep, I make my way down the hall to the bathroom, take care of business, then feel my way up the stairs. The hall light is off, meaning that Mom is still at the hospital with Kyle. She always leaves the light on when she goes to bed in case my dad decides to stumble home in the middle of the night, which he rarely does. I make it a point to shut the light off when Mom isn't here.

I step into the kitchen and turn on the light. I pour myself a glass of water from the jug in the fridge and begin to drink. Between swallows I think I hear something. I pause. Nothing. I finish the glass of water and pour another. Just as I close the refrigerator door, I hear the noise again. A low moan, like someone is asleep. Or drunk.

My dad's here.

I tiptoe into the living room and, although my eyes haven't yet adjusted to the dark, I think I see the shape of my father's body on the couch. He is still making the low moaning sound. I step right up to the couch and look down at him.

It's not my father. It's Mom.

Why would she come home and leave Kyle alone at the hospital? She knows how scared he gets. My eyes finally adjust and I see that she has her back turned to me and is sobbing quietly into a pillow.

"Ma?"

She doesn't hear me.

"Ma? Are you okay?"

She takes a deep breath, lets out a long sigh, and keeps sobbing.

"Ma, what's going on? Where's Kyle?"

She pulls her face out of the pillow and turns toward me slowly. A shaft of light from a streetlamp falls on her face and I see her dark, sunken eyes and wet cheeks. Her hair looks damp and sticks to her face.

"Gone," she says.

"Gone where, Ma?"

"He's gone."

She's not making any sense.

"What do you mean 'gone,' Ma?" I ask. "Where is he?"

She answers, and I think maybe I don't hear her right. It sounded like she said "dead."

"What happened to Kyle, Mom?"

"He's dead, Jake."

A glowing ball of heat starts in my stomach and makes its way up my chest until I'm sure that I'm going to be sick. Mom turns away and buries her face in the pillow. I stand over her in the dark and say nothing for a long time.

Chapter 4

I wake up on the living room floor and the sun is shining in my eyes. Mom is snoring loudly on the couch, her body still curled into a ball, her hands and feet tucked between the cushions. Her eyes are swollen and her cheeks look red and soft.

The clock on the VCR says 8:47. Shit. I'm supposed to be at work, opening the store. I pick up the phone to call and remember that no one is there. My mind's eye drums up a picture of customers lined up around the block, pounding the door and repeating some ridiculous chant. Maybe they'll burn an effigy of a 16-year-old kid in a blue and red polo shirt. The name tag would clearly read "Jacob." Or maybe Yellow Girl is standing doe-eyed outside the store, desperately needing a pack of smokes. Or maybe . . .

My brother is dead.

It hits me like a kick in the chest. I'm suddenly light-headed, so I back up to the nearest chair and sit. My head seems so full it could burst, but everything moves so quickly that I can't grasp a single thought. My breath is gone. No one close to me has ever died, and I don't know the right way to react. I purse my lips and squint my eyes and push, hoping to bring tears. But I can't cry. I feel a sense of loss, but it doesn't seem real.

Damn it, I think. *My brother is dead. Why can't I cry? I cried at the end of E.T. for fuck's sake, I cried when Grandma's old dog, Fussy, died. Why can't I cry now?*

I decide to go back to bed, and while I'm walking down the stairs, I'm aware suddenly that I'm intentionally dragging my feet and hanging my head, like I think someone with a dead brother should. I try to force myself to think only of Kyle, of him suffering and dying in a bright white hospital room, of his tiny body clothed in a suit and tie, lying wax-faced in a coffin with his lips sewn shut, but my mind wanders to Yellow Girl, to my job, to the upcoming school year. *What the hell is wrong with me?* I wonder. *My brother is dead. What the hell is wrong with me?*

Just Jake | 27

I lie down in bed, but my room is too bright to sleep. There's a softness in the air that I can't explain. A subtle smell that's not quite flowers has settled in the room and my sheets feel soothingly cool. A ladybug on the ceiling catches my attention. Even if I squint, I can't count its spots. It moves in confusing little jerking motions, stops at what seems random times, then turns and scurries in a different direction. I wonder what it's looking for, where it's going. I hear a faint buzz like a thin, vibrating reed as its shiny orange shell splits and lifts like suicide doors to unsheathe delicately veined wings, trembling as if to fly. But it doesn't move. It makes a deliberate ninety-degree turn and again shakes its thin wings, then falls and I hear an audible *thwip* as it lands on my bedspread.

Sitting up, I scour the bedspread with narrowed eyes, hoping to detect movement. I see nothing except brown sprigs of yarn and awkward-shaped stars and rectangles cut from favorite shirts from my childhood. I could get up to turn on the light but I'm afraid to move, afraid I'll crush that smooth orange shell, the fragile wings beneath. Again I hear the faint buzz, the vibration of those slender wings. The sound rises slowly, level with my chest, then chin, until finally I make out the dark spot of the ladybug, silhouetted against my bedroom's ivory walls. The buzzing grows fainter, trailing off into silence as the insect disappears into the corner of my room.

I drag myself up the stairs around supper time, and Mom is sitting at the dining room table in a pink robe. Her hair is flat on one side and her cheeks sag like dough. Her eyes look sunken, exhausted, held up by puffy half-moons the color of bruised plums. She holds her knees together, the lower half of her left leg jutting to one side. Her foot is turned inward, her toes curling and uncurling. Her right hand and elbow rest on the table, while her left hand grips a handful of pink fabric in her lap. She breathes deeply and slowly, her bottom lip curling out with each exhale. If her eyes weren't open, I would think she was asleep.

In the kitchen, a pile of dirty plates and bowls leans toward the scuffed floor. The air smells of burnt coffee.

A shiny black cricket makes its way across the linoleum and climbs up onto the dining room carpet. Antennae spiraling, it darts across the floor and onto my mother's right foot, flat and motionless under the table. It crosses the thin skin of her foot, stretched over bluish veins. Mom doesn't seem to notice. Her lip rolls in and out, steady as a miniature tide.

I need to get out of the house. The moment I step outside, I'm struck by the humidity. Each breath feels like I'm swallowing a wet cloth. Waves of heat dance over the street, fogging and twisting the power plant in the distance as it pumps black smoke into the sky, marring the clean, white clouds to a dull grey.

I grab my bike from the garage and set off down the street. I can see the Big Tree in the distance, another block up and around the corner. It rises high above the trees around it, only the bare lower half of its trunk obstructed, its thick branches reaching out and up like the arms of a meditative congregation. The Big Tree is a place I've liked to go since I was little. My dad always said that someone in my family owned the land around it—some sister of my grandmother's that lived in Las Vegas. I imagine her surrounded by flashing marquees, the air polluted by incessant car horns. She has a tall, orange, beehive hairdo and too much bright red lipstick. I've never understood why she would buy a little plot of land on the edge of a town like this, almost clear across the continent from her home. Had she ever even seen the land? I doubted it. Maybe her high-rolling friends are impressed when she casually mentions her "plot of wilderness in upstate Minnesota," which is what I imagine she calls it, pinky finger jutting deliberately from a thin-stemmed glass.

I pull my bike up the curb, walk it down the small grassy slope, and lean it against the Tree. Once, when we were much younger, five of us held hands and tried to encircle the massive trunk. We made it about 2/3 around. At the bottom of the slope stands the surprisingly intact remains of a fort some friends and I built years ago out of straw bales from my grandpa's farm. We stacked the bales three high into a long, narrow hallway ending in a larger open room. The roof, a series of rotting wooden planks laid across the bales, had been almost high enough that we could stand inside at the time. Crawling inside now, I find that I can't quite kneel without lifting a plank with my head. I sit, settling against one of the bales and breathe in the musty smell. The straw pokes my back through my shirt.

In one corner, I see a fat brown spider hanging motionless in a perfectly formed web. Illuminated by a strip of light leaking in between two roof planks, it sparkles like wet glass.

A voice outside startles me and I sit up, lifting a roof plank enough that I can see the Big Tree and the slope running alongside. Two voices, both male. Laughing. Definitely getting closer. One of the voices sounds like Darrell, a skinny, red-haired kid from my school. The other I don't recognize, but it sounds older, confident. Both of them eventually come into view over the slope, first a blue baseball cap and a mess of reddish hair, then both faces, eyes squinting from the bright summer sun. It is him—Darrell Oakes—and some other guy I don't recognize. He's tall and broad-shouldered but kind of toady-looking. A football player type. Darrell's my age but the other guy looks older, probably a Tech School-er.

"Did you, though?" Darrell asks.

"Did I what?" the other guy says.

"You know what," answers Darrell. "Did you, like, get in her pants?"

"Yeah, I got in her pants," the other guys answers. "What did you think we were doing in there?"

"What was it like?" Darrell asks.

"What do you mean, what was it like?" the other guy says. "It was like what it was always like. Except kind of better, 'cause, you know, it's been a while."

"So is this gonna be, like, a regular thing again or what?" Darrell asks.

"How the hell would I know?" the other guy says. "Be cool if it was. I got nothin' else goin' on." They're a little ways down the street now and I can barely hear them. Darrell punches the other guy lightly in the arm right before their heads dip behind the curb, out of view.

Chapter 5

The next day I show up at work around quarter to four and act like nothing happened. My boss is standing behind the counter with his back turned; I count three separate rolls of fat on the back of his neck. I duck into the break room, hoping he leaves before I take over the till. I wasn't the only one scheduled yesterday and I didn't get a phone call, so I'm desperately holding onto the possibility that he doesn't know I wasn't here.

The break room table is covered with celebrity magazines and fashion journals. I pick up an issue with a bikini-clad waif on the cover and turn to an article that promises *101 Ways to Spice up your Sex Life!* What a frickin' joke. I continue to rifle through the magazines until a newspaper catches my eye. The cover has a story about some vote on a tax or something that I couldn't possibly care less about. I'm turning through the pages, scanning for the crossword, when I happen upon a black-and-white picture of my brother. I'm confused for a second before it hits me: his obituary. It's still real. My brother is still dead. It wasn't some sick Candid Camera joke that Mom played. It's right in front of my face: *Kyle Withers, age 10 of Browerton, Minnesota . . . youngest son of Patty and Calvin . . . older brother Jacob . . . funeral services to be held . . .*

I fold up the paper and toss it to the very corner of the table, as far away as I can get it.

The clock on the microwave says 3:52. I take a few deep breaths and sneak over to the door, peeking out the window into the store. My boss is standing in the candy aisle with a package of *Starburst* in his hand. He stares at it like he's waiting for it to talk to him or something. His white dress shirt barely holds back his sizable gut; the spaces between the buttons are pulled open, revealing a yellowish undershirt. His belly hangs over the front of his belt and his underarms are marked with huge, wet circles. He raises his eyebrows suddenly, squares his shoulders and walks toward the door, pausing to say something to Geoff, who is

Just Jake | 31

obviously more than ready for me to take over the till. He disappears out the door.

I open the break room door far enough to stick my head out: "Is he gone gone, or just a little while gone?"

Geoff, startled, takes a deep breath before replying. "Geez, dude. I didn't see you there. You scared the shit outta me," he says. "Yeah, he's gone."

"Did he ask about me?" I creep out of the break room, still a little wary. "I mean, about where I was yesterday?"

"No," says Geoff. "Why, were you supposed to be here?"

"Yeah. Couldn't make it. Something came up." I throw on my red QuikMart visor and step behind the counter, as ready as I'll get for another day.

"You punched in?" Geoff asks.

"Yeah," I say. "Get outta here."

My mom walks into the store around 6:30, which is kind of weird for two reasons. One, she never comes to this store and two, she never misses *Wheel of Fortune*. She walks past the counter looking at her feet and she doesn't see me. She moves with a slow shuffle. Her hair is laid flat into a big, round spot on the back of her head like she just got out of bed. At the back of the store she opens a cooler door and takes out a jug of milk. She's wearing her light blue fuzzy slippers. She plods back to the front of the store, grabs a box of some kind of kids' cereal on the way. She steps to the counter, still looking at her feet.

"Hey Ma," I say. She looks up, a bit startled but still languid.

"Oh," she says. "Oh."

"It's nice to see you, Ma," I say, ringing up her milk and cereal. "How's your . . . uh . . . how are you doing?"

"Oh, I'm fine, Jake. We're doing good. We watched some *Scoobie Doo* today and then Kylie was hungry and we didn't have any cereal. So I came to get some. Some cereal." I don't know if she's trying to make some kind of joke or what. If she is, it isn't funny.

"What do you mean, Mom?" I ask. "What do you mean, you and Kyle? Kyle is gone, Mom. His funeral is in a couple days." Her eyes narrow for a moment and her bottom lip curls. The black-and-white photo from the paper flashes in my mind, and I push it away.

"Jake. Why would you say that, Jake? Why would you say that about your little brother? He loves you so much, you know. He can't really show it, but he does."

Oh, God. She doesn't know. Somehow, she doesn't remember or doesn't believe or something. She's sick again. Worse than I've ever seen her. As sick as Dad said.

A woman walks into the store and I glare at her. Wish her away. I need to talk to Mom. I need to do something.

"Mom, I don't know what . . ." I say. "Kyle died, Mom. At the hospital. You told me he did. You were with him, Mom. You were there. Don't you . . .?" She looks up at me and smiles. She blushes a little and turns her head to the side playfully, waves her hand at me, dismissing what I said.

"You coot. You really are a coot, Jake." She picks up her milk and cereal and shuffles out the door without her change. I want to run out the door after her, shake her and tell her the truth. Make her believe. But I know I can't. What Dad said was true—she really can get that sick, and she is. Nothing I can say will matter. I don't even know how much longer she'll know who I am.

My mind is gone for the rest of the shift. All I can think about is Mom and what I should do about her. Is she sitting at home right now watching cartoons, a bowl of soggy cereal sitting untouched on the tray of Kyle's empty wheelchair? Is she talking to him? Does she see him there next to her, smell his unwashed hair, hear his thick, phlegmy, gurgle of a laugh? His funeral is on Monday, just a couple days away. His obituary was in today's paper, for God's sake.

The little brass bell on the door rings and I look up to see the chubby penguin girl come through the door and smile at me. She's wearing a tee shirt this time, but still has the green flip-flops on. She clumsily ambles up to the counter, grinning like she's getting her picture taken.

"Hi, Jake," she says. "Or Jacob." I'm not really sure what to say. "Your name tag," she continues, pointing to my chest. "It says 'Jacob,' but I know people call you 'Jake.' Jackie calls you 'Jaker,' which I think is cute."

"Jackie?" I ask, confused.

"Yeah," she says. "My friend. She was in here with me. Curly blonde hair. I thought you guys were friends."

"Oh, Jackie," I say. "I . . . uh . . . didn't know her name. I mean, she never actually told me." I'm realizing how stupid that sounds when it occurs to me that she said 'friends.' "So . . . she talks about me? She said we were friends?"

"Yeah, she said you guys were friends," the girl answers. "She doesn't *talk* about you exactly, but she said that she saw you here the other night. I'm Megan, by the way. Funny that I can keep talking without remembering to even tell someone my name. It's Megan."

"You already said that," I say.

"Oh," she says, and smiles again.

Just Jake | 33

"Anyway, Jackie was wondering what you're doing after work tonight," she says. "She wants to know if it's okay if she meets you in the parking lot again."

I can literally feel my heart speed up in my chest and my breath quickens almost into gasps. Little bugs buzz around in my brain and a million possibilities of what tonight might hold rush through my head all at once.

"I'm not busy," I say. "She can meet me here."

"Great," says Megan. "I'll tell her. See you, Jake." She does something with her eye that's not quite a wink before she turns and lopes back out the door. The shift was dragging slowly enough already, with my mind refusing to focus on anything but Mom and that picture of Kyle, my brother, now nothing more than a grainy photograph, a collection of tiny black dots on shitty grey paper. Now I'm almost sick with excitement and anxiety and I can't help but glance at the clock every five minutes. I push Mom and Kyle as far away as my brain will let me and try to drum up a picture of Jackie in my mind, but I can't. Can't even remember what she looks like. Something won't let me.

I've managed to get all my closing duties done early—or mostly done, anyway—and I'm ready to leave the store by a little after midnight. I stop in the break room quick to get rid of my visor (I refuse to even bring it outside the store), and a knot forms in my stomach, thick and heavy. The newspaper is sprawled out on the table, open to my brother's obituary. Kyle's messy hair and crooked teeth, his neck tilted awkwardly to one side like something from a Gustav Klimt painting, his eyes black, lifeless. I want to crumple the paper up and throw it away, convince myself that it's not him, never was him. Instead, I take a deep breath and carefully tear the picture out. I drag my fingertips across it, and the ink smears a little, stains my fingers black. The paper feels fragile and dry as I fold it up and shove it in the front pocket of my jeans.

As I'm walking through the parking lot, I look up and see Jackie leaning against the door of my car, smoking a cigarette. "Hey!" she calls out while I'm still a good 50 yards away. "Hey!" I call back, and my voice is not mine. As I approach, she turns her head and blows a smoke ring, which disappears in the wind. Her short, black skirt flutters to one side and the wind has draped her blonde curls over her left shoulder, partially obscuring the low 'V' of her tight, black sweater. A black, pin-striped newsboy hat casts a curved shadow over most of her face.

"Give me your keys," she says, expressionless, and extends her hand, palm up.

My face must ask the question, because she speaks again before I do: "I'm driving." Intrigued, I hand them over.

"Right this way," she says, and leads me to a dark area of the parking lot and her waiting car—a light blue sporty number, older. Nothing too fancy, but a definite step up from my Pinto.

"Nice car," I say. "Is it yours?"

"Mm hmm." She opens the driver's door and hits the unlock button.

"I don't get it," I say. "Why did you take my keys?" Her face crinkles a little, and she chews her lower lip.

"You're not going to need them." She shrugs a little, slides into the car, and closes the door. I climb in too, settling into the leather bucket seat.

"Where we going?"

"You'll see," she replies, smiling. The engine sputters a little before it turns over, and the car's tires squawk as she pulls out of the Quik-Mart parking lot and onto Main Street.

"I actually gotta be home pretty soon," I say.

"Why?" she asks. "Mommy give you a curfew?" She glances at me, then looks back to the road.

"No," I say. "I got something I need to do."

"I'll get you home safe, Jaker," she says. "Relax."

We pass only two cars as we cross town and turn onto Swinden Strip, the winding road that runs the length of Rockwell Lake, the road that will carry us out of Browerton and onto the starlit country roads of Rockwell County.

Chapter 6

"Your friend Megan came into the store today," I say, fidgeting nervously with the buckle of my seatbelt. On the radio, Sting pleads to Roxanne not to wear that dress tonight.

"I know," says Jackie.

"She told me your name."

"Yeah?" she says.

"I didn't know it before," I say. "I mean, I don't think you ever told me." She pushes the clutch and shifts into fifth gear like a NASCAR racer, her hand jerking forward, a confident blur.

"What's in a name," she says, stating more than asking. "It's actually Jacqueline, but nobody really calls me that unless they want a black eye. Not that I've ever given someone one." She hits the brake pedal and swerves a little to avoid a squirrel on the road. "You drink, Jake?"

"Sure do," I say, adjusting my seat a little. "Actually, I could really go for one right now. You have no idea."

Jackie leans back and reaches her right arm behind her seat. "Know it's here somewhere," she mumbles, her hand fumbling blindly. "Aha!" and she pulls out a liter bottle. "Whiskey," she says, anticipating my question. She unscrews the cap, slugs quickly from the bottle, and wipes her mouth with her forearm. She hands me the bottle, still uncapped. I tip it back for a three count—sort of my starting ritual for a straight-from-the-bottle night—and hand it back to her.

"You always keep a bottle of whiskey in your car?" I ask.

"Nope," she says. "Sort of borrowed it from my dad. This stuff is like thirty bucks a bottle." An old van with one headlight passes us—the first vehicle we've seen since leaving town. "I've got ice and Diet Coke in the trunk if you wanna mix. I'm gonna mix one when we get there," she says. "I've got some beers, too, if you're into that." She takes another small pull from the bottle and shakes her a head couple times, hard. "*Blechh.* That stuff's nasty straight." I lean over a little and reach my hand out.

35

She gives me the bottle. I tip it back and drink again, this time only a two count.

"Any requests?" Jackie asks.

"Huh?"

"Music. Anything you want to hear?" She flips open the armrest between us. It's full of cassette tapes. "No CD player, but I've got some pretty good tapes." She glances at me quick and smiles. "If I do say so myself."

I pull out a stack and shuffle through them. *REM, Sunny Day Real Estate, Sonic Youth, The Clash, Sepultura.* "Quite a selection," I say. "I'm impressed. Some really good stuff here." I pop in Faith No More's *Angel Dust.*

"Ah," she says. "Good choice."

I hand the bottle back to Jackie and already I can feel my brain getting fuzzy. The stripes on the road come at me at varying speeds, sometimes slowly, frame-by-frame, and then, suddenly, whizzing by, a fat yellow blur. I try to focus on the rhythm of the yellow lines to keep Kyle out of my head, but he keeps creeping in. *Where is he now? Laying on a cold, steel table, covered with a white blanket? In a morgue drawer, a tag on his toe?* My mind refuses to put his face anywhere but in that one photograph, the only Kyle that seems real to me now. I reach into my pocket and flatten my hand over Kyle's picture; the edges of the paper poke my hand. I tuck my thumb under it and hold it against my palm.

Jackie lights a cigarette. Offers me one.

"No thanks," I say. "Don't smoke, remember? Not cigarettes, at least. I'd spark a joint if you had one." My voice comes out in weird bubbles that start in my throat, grow, and then pop in the air as they come out my mouth.

"'Fraid not," she says, and she turns her head to look at me. Smiles. "I think the turn's coming up. Second right after this sign." She points her chin toward a wooden plank nailed to a fence post. Crappy painting of Donald Duck jumping off a high dive with an inner tube around his waist, palms pressed together like he's praying not to break his neck. *Welcome Point,* it says.

She swerves the car into the right turn lane. Doesn't use her blinker. We turn onto a highway with no shoulder, a steep hill that turns to gravel as we reach the top, and then begin a long plunge into a deep valley.

"I've never been on this road before," I say.

"I was counting on that, Jaker," she says, and flashes me that killer smile again. I swear to God my heart hurts. The road plummets deeper and deeper. We pass a black cow standing surprisingly close to the road. I swear I see the striations of its jaw muscles as it chews its cud. I catch a glimpse of something in the field behind the cow. A massive grey formation that twinkles in spots. I squint my eyes for a better look, but the bright shaft of the headlights cuts past it and back into the tall grass before I get a good look.

The car slows, and Jackie turns off the road and onto a small dirt approach, little more than two tire ruts with grass in between.

"Well," she says. "We're here."

Chapter 7

She opens the trunk and struggles to pull out a huge, red cooler. I offer to help and she steps aside as I lift the cooler and set it on the gravel behind the car.

"This thing weighs a ton," I say. "What's in here?"

"I already told you," she says. "Have a look." I open the lid, and the inside of the cooler is stacked with carefully placed cans of beer and a few cans of coke. A bag of ice rests on top of the cans.

"You sure came prepared, huh?" I say, and she smiles. Lights up another cigarette. "Are we bringing this out there?" I ask, and tilt my head toward the field. "It doesn't have wheels."

"We'll each take a side," she says. "Unless you need me to take it myself, little man." She shoots me an adorable grin and bends over to grab one of the cooler's handles. The moonlight isn't quite bright enough for me to see if bending over pulled her skirt up far enough to reveal her underwear, which I imagine is black like her skirt. Red would be okay, too. I throw the whiskey bottle into the cooler and grab the other handle.

"Lead the way." We walk through the ditch and duck under a fence, me on one side of the cooler, Jackie on the other. She mentions twice that the tall grass makes her legs itch, and both times she stops to scratch them. I can just make out the shape of the formation in the distance, little more than a dull, grey mirage in the foggy black.

"What is this place?" I ask.

"A field," she answers. I don't know if I'm supposed to laugh.

Jackie steps ahead of me, so we're walking more or less single file, and the long grass gives way to what feels like a rudimentary path of packed dirt. The grey shape looms larger as we approach, a lone monolith standing guard in the otherwise featureless field. My eyes strain as I try to make sense of its size, its shape. My mind struggles in the darkness to give it shapes and features that I'm sure it could not have. It isn't until we're close enough that the gigantic shape blocks out the moon and I reach out my hand to touch the cold, rough surface that I realize what it is: a giant formation of stone, probably granite, that, in my mind, has no business rising up randomly out of a pasture in rural Minnesota, the middle of nowhere.

We set the cooler down and I walk along the massive rock, grazing my fingertips against its sharp edges.

"This is nuts," I say. "Fucking crazy. I've never seen anything like this."

"Yeah," Jackie says. "I like it here. You can really see the stars."

"You come here a lot?"

"That trail is mostly mine." She opens the cooler lid and pulls out a sleeve of plastic cups. Hands me one. "You want to mix your own or you want me to do it?"

"The bottle's fine with me," I say. "For now, at least." I tip the bottle and drink deeply, deeper than I would normally. She's watching. She throws a few ice cubes in a glass. Mixes what appears to be a fairly strong drink. Grabs a crag edge with both hands, pulls herself up and smooths out her skirt. Peeks at me quick, then blows a thick blonde curl out of her eye with the corner of her mouth.

"It's so nice out," she says. "Such a beautiful night."

"Yeah," I say. And it is. *Not as beautiful as you are*, I want to say, but know better. I'm not that drunk. Yet. I slug from the bottle again and cap it. Setting it on the ledge next to Jackie, I pull myself up and sit a few feet from her. Somewhere in the field a cricket chirps a steady, lulling rhythm. I want to ask her why she brought me here, but I'm afraid it's a question that would seem hopelessly out of place. This rock, these stars, the swaying grass, the cricket. It should all be enough. My head swims and without even deciding to, I scoot closer to her on the rock ledge. The wind ripples the front of her skirt a little, and I almost reach over to smooth it out.

"What're you thinking about?" she asks suddenly, leaning back against the granite. I want to tell her that I'm thinking about my dead brother, whose wheelchair sits in my living room like a tombstone. Or my crazy mom who doesn't seem to know he's dead and can't even manage to shower or get dressed anymore. I want to tell her that my brother is dead and I don't even know if my father knows. I want to tell her that she's probably better off forgetting that she ever met me because, in reality, I may not be as fucked up as they are yet, but I will be. My brother is dead and I can't even cry. I drink and I forget that he's even gone. I picture him at home, sitting at the table in his wheelchair, and mom's feeding him and he's gurgling and laughing and she's laughing and has a spark of life in her eyes that only exists during these times and that I may never see again. I want to reach into my pocket and take out the wrinkled, fuzzy, black and white photo that is the only brother I have left and show it to her. "*That's my brother!*" I want to yell. "*See him? Look at him! He's dead! I no longer have a brother, it's been years since I've had a father, and I don't know how much is left of my mother. So don't get close to me. Don't let me get close to you. I will envelope you like a storm. I will wrap my life around yours and never let go, because I don't fucking have anyone left. You are beautiful, you are real, and for whatever reason, you have chosen to be here with me, right now. I barely know you, but you might be the only thing I have left.*"

"Not gonna tell me?" she asks, and slides back on the ledge, crossing her legs under her.

"Nothing, I guess," I say. Then, "My brother's dead."

"What?" she asks.

"Yeah," I say, and reach for the bottle again. My head and stomach feel hot and bubbly. "A couple days ago. He, uh . . . . he died."

"I . . ." she begins, then stops. Squints her eyes at me and chews her lower lip. "I don't know . . ."

"He was sick, I guess," I say. "He was ten. His name was Kyle. He was always sick, but . . .," and I sound like I'm reasoning, trying to convince myself of something.

She scoots closer to me and leans in. Puts her arm around me and lays her head on my shoulder like she thinks I might cry. The wind blows a thick blonde curl against my neck. The moonlight is bright enough that I can make out the smooth curves of her cleavage less than a foot away from my face, and I hate myself for thinking things like that because my brother is dead.

"I'm sorry I abducted you tonight, Jake," Jackie says. "You should probably be at home with your family, huh? Do you want me to take you home?" I start to tell her that I barely have a family, but I stumble over my words. I can't figure out what to say, so I make up a lie about my mother and father leaving town to pick up an elderly relative for Kyle's funeral. "So really, it's a good thing that you abducted me tonight," I say. "Otherwise, I'd be sitting at home by myself watching T.V. and getting high."

"I thought you said you didn't have any weed."

"I don't have any on me," I say. I start to say that I usually steal it from my old man, and I catch myself just in time and tell her that I have some at home. I decide that I'd like for Jackie to think my life is as normal as hers for as long as possible.

"I'm glad I don't have to take you home yet, Jake," she says, and she looks up at me and smiles. "There's something here that I want to show you, but we won't be able to see it until the sun comes up." I ask her if she intends for us to be here until then, and she tells me that there are two sleeping bags in the back seat of her car. I get that feeling again in my chest—the one where my heart kind of hurts—and I realize that I really need to kiss this girl. I need to do it right now or I may never, ever have another chance. A beautiful, smart, and interesting girl who is two years my senior is drunk, has her head on my shoulder, and intends to spend the night with me. If there's one thing ol' Jake is good at, it's messing things like this up.

I realize suddenly that Jackie's head is no longer on my shoulder, and before I even look up, she has leaped from the ledge and is standing below me, offering both hands to help me down. Damn.

"Come on," she says. "Let's go for a walk. There's a little pond over here and we should go get the sleeping bags anyway."

On our way back to the car we detour off the path and Jackie leads us to a small pond; it's difficult to see exactly how large it is in the dark, but it appears to be smaller than a football field.

"I bet we can find a good spot to sleep over here," she says, and runs ahead with her arms in front of her, pushing thick reeds out of the way. The tips of the cattails break apart and the cottony white seeds float into the air, tickling my nose.

"This is perfect!" Jackie yells from a dozen or so yards ahead of me. "Check this out, Jake!"

When I get to where she is standing, I see that she has found a small clearing in the cattails, probably a deer bed. "We can lay the sleeping bags right here," Jackie says. "We'll have protection in case the wind picks up and we can still see the stars from here."

"We'll have protection from mountain lions, too," I joke, and I can't even pretend to laugh because I see Kyle in my head again. My hand absently travels into my pocket and clutches the photo of him, making sure that it's real. I need another shot badly but we left the bottle back at the rock. "I'm going to run and grab the booze," I say, turning and taking off at a jog. Then, over my shoulder: "I'll be right back." She asks if I need help but I pretend not to hear.

The air feels thick and wet in my lungs as I jog back to the cooler, and I can feel the dew on the grass wetting my shoes through to my socks. The booze has altered my reflexes considerably and running across the bumpy ground proves a challenge. Several times I duck and swerve and nearly lose my footing. I can't seem to find the path we took earlier, but I can see the granite formation in the distance, cutting a rough bite out of the bottom half of the crescent moon.

When I reach the rock, the cooler is sitting on the grass at its base and I reach up to the ledge where we had sat, feeling in the shadows for the whiskey bottle. I can't find it; it must have fallen to the ground when we jumped from the ledge. Pulling my lighter from my pocket, I flick the flame on and crouch down, scouring the ground for the bottle. The lighter's weak orange glow creates wispy, dancing shadows, inkblack demons, hunched and broad-shouldered, that breathe and pulsate on the rock and in the grass, demons made more vicious and real by the liquor swimming in my stomach, clouding my mind.

The swath of dull light falls on a section of the giant rock a few feet off the ground, and I glimpse a jagged white line on the rough surface. Then another. And another.

I kneel and bring the lighter closer to the chalk-like etchings and, squinting and leaning close, I can barely make out the rudimentary shape of a horse, etched cave painting-style on the rock face. Its back legs are bent, front legs raised off the ground, arched menacingly in a classic "Hi-ho, Silver, away!" pose. Its tail and mane—the only parts that have been drawn painstakingly and filled in white—flow out behind the horse in sharp, wavy points, and suddenly I am at home in my living room with Kyle while he gurgles at the T.V., a Wells Fargo commercial playing on the screen. A team of majestic brown horses pulls a stagecoach down a narrow, dusty road that leads off into a sunset, and Kyle shifts excitedly in his chair, his deep, rusty laugh bubbling from his throat. I go to Kyle and lean down to him. I put my arm around his shoulder and pull myself close to him, burying my face in the back of his neck. I feel his warm drool on my neck and I hold him as tight as I can, whisper in his ear that I won't let him go; I'll never, ever let him go.

Then I'm drifting, being pulled from this moment back into the breezy night at the foot of the giant rock. The night and everything in it have become soft and hazy, the shadows less threatening but every bit as real. Stumbling backward, I step on something hard, lose my footing, and trip. A few feet to my left, the crescent moon reflects off of the whiskey bottle I'd been looking for. I uncap it, tip it back all the way to twelve o'clock. The whiskey burns my throat and settles in my stomach like a burned-out star. I lean back and lay my head on the cool ground. A squeaking sound comes to me on the breeze, distant but familiar. I close my eyes tight, trying to will it away. I shake my head from side to side hard; blades of dry, yellowed grass poke my ears and the sides of my face. The sound grows increasingly louder, ebbing and flowing with the gusts of wind, and I press my palms to my ears and hum like a child trying to ignore his mother. But the high-pitched, metallic squeal grows louder and louder until I know that if I open my eyes, I will see my dead brother wheeling toward me, slumped in his chair as invisible hands roll it across the packed ground.

Hands still pressed to my ears, I sit up and struggle to my knees, then stand and run in the direction of Jackie and the pond. I run for five full seconds before I open my eyes and even then I only flick them open in short bursts to make sure I'm not about to run headlong into a tree or sprain my ankle in a woodchuck hole. Twice I trip and fall before I reach the pond and Jackie, seated cross-legged in the clearing smoking a cigarette.

"What's up?" she asks. "Where's the whiskey?"

I struggle to answer between deep, choked breaths, but I'm not even sure what to say.

"Jake?" she asks. "You okay?" She pushes herself to her feet and walks toward me.

"I need . . . to go . . . home," I tell her. "Now."

"Okaaaaay," she says. "But your family's not even home, Jake."

"I know," I say. "Or . . . . maybe they are. I . . . need to go . . . home now."

"I'm too drunk to drive, Jake," she says. "I was planning to stay here 'til morning, remember?" She steps closer to me and puts her hand on my shoulder.

"Then I'll drive," I say. "You can stay at my house if you want."

Walking back to the rock to grab the cooler, Jackie speaks several times but I barely hear her words—cannot fully make sense of what she's asking me. My brother's face in crinkled, grey newspaper plays through my head over and over again like a moment when I said the wrong thing and only later came up with a snappy comeback. Jackie quiets and in silence we carry the cooler back to the car, where she hands me her keys. We strap in for the starlit drive home.

Chapter 8

It's nearly 4:00 a.m. and the house is dark when I pull into the driveway and park Jackie's car on the patch of yellow grass next to the garage. I've turned the engine off and removed my seatbelt before I realize that I could have just parked in the driveway; Mom will not be going to work tomorrow. Mom's car will probably be in the garage for a very long time. In the sudden silence I hear the faint sound of Jackie snoring. Sometimes when I drive drunk I feel like I own the road. Like nothing can stop me. Tonight, though, I crept along the highway, both hands tightly gripping the wheel. I hadn't even noticed Jackie falling asleep.

"Jackie," I whisper, facing her as I kneel on the driver's seat. "Psst. Wake up."

She inhales sharply, then exhales through her open mouth, a raspy sound coming from her throat. I put my hand on her shoulder and shake her, gently at first, then harder.

"Hey, Jackie," I say, louder this time. "Wake up. We're at my house. You can sleep on the couch."

Again she doesn't stir. The moonlight cuts a smoky blue crescent across her pale skin. Her bottom lip pulses in and out with each snoring breath. Her hat has slipped off her head and rests on her shoulder, wedged between her neck and the car window. Her left hand lies palm up on her thigh, curled as though accepting an offering.

I don't know how long I look at her, taking in each soft curve of her body: the back of her arm, the inside of her thigh, the mound of each breast. She adjusts in her seat and I watch her skirt pull up, her bare legs falling into a patch of blue-tinted moonlight. Instinctively, I reach over to readjust her skirt, to cover her. My fingertips brush the cool flesh of her thigh and I'm suddenly aware that my lips are chapped, dry and cracked as parched soil. I move my hand up and down her leg slowly, drag my knuckles across the curve of her inner thigh. She mutters sleepily under her breath but doesn't stir. Slowly and smoothly I caress her thigh, bringing my hand down to her knee, then back up. I watch my hand disappear under her skirt. My fingers find her warmth and I slide closer to her on the seat. Pressing my face to her neck I breathe in her smell. Her long blonde curls tickle my nose and cheeks and I curl my fingers over her warmth, feeling her, holding her.

A car turns onto the block and its headlights fall on my face. Sliding back to the driver's seat, I open the door and step out. I stand and realize just how drunk I really am, just how stupid it was for me to be driving. Crossing the driveway to the other side of the car, I open the door and catch Jackie in my arms as she slumps out of her seat, and toward the pavement. She is surprisingly light as I pick her up and carry her into my house and down to the basement, where I splay her out on the couch and pull a blanket over her. I lie down on the floor next to her and fall asleep to the sound of a ringing that may or may not be in my ears.

Some time later—it must have been fewer than two hours, as the night sky has just begun to accept the pale blue of morning—I am awakened by a nightmare I can't remember. I am still drunk, but have the presence of mind to realize that I would like to get Jackie out of my house before she has a chance to meet my mother. She snores loudly on the couch next to me, her limbs cocked at unnatural angles. She won't be awake for hours.

I turn on the small lamp on the end table and wait for my eyes to adjust to the light before making my way up the stairs and down the hall to my mother's room. Her door is wide open and the faint light of the breaking dawn reveals the shape of her body, dressed in her pink robe, on the bed, the comforter still tucked under the mattress. She breathes softly and rhythmically while a small fan hums, oscillating at her bedside. I feel a strong urge to lie down next to my mother, to hold her in my arms so that we can wake up together and I can try to tell her that things will be okay. She looks young in this low light, the deep wrinkles of her face and dry, greying hairs hidden in shadow. Her appearance betrays the signs of stress and aging that mark her skin, her eyes, her hands.

Leaning down gently, I sweep aside a lock of my mother's hair that clings damply to her face and kiss her forehead. I turn to leave the room and I'm in the hallway when I hear her voice.

"Jake?" she asks quietly. Her voice is soft and awkward. The voice of a pubescent boy. I turn back to her and step into the room.

"Yeah, Ma?"

"Do me a kindness, honey," she says.

"Sure, Ma," I say. "What?"

"Stay outta the bars, Jake," she says. "And stay away from girls. You're too young. You're just a baby. And what about your family, Jake? Don't you think they need you? Your wife and your sons? What about them, honey? They need you at home."

"Sure, Ma." *I'm sorry you're so sick, Mom.* I don't speak the words. I just think them really hard, sort of send them to her. *I wish I knew what to do to help you, Mom, but I don't.*

In the basement, Jackie is still asleep. I lower myself onto the couch near her feet and watch her chest rise and fall, listening to the tide of her breathing. I wonder what kind of mother Jackie would be. A girl as smart as she is could never turn out like my Mom. A girl as smart as she is would know exactly, instinctively, what her children need. She would know when they are happy, when they are sad. She would know when they are invisible and how and where to find them. And she would sure as hell know if one of them was dead. Or if both of them were.

Chapter 9

"Jake?"

I slowly open my eyes, still glued shut by sleep, and someone is shaking me. My mouth and throat feel like sandpaper and my head is pounding.

"Jake. Wake up." Through sleep-blurred eyes I'm able to make out the shape of my mother. Her head is a wild silhouette against the grey light of the living room, a bird's nest of hair and bobby pins. I prop up on my elbows and turn toward her, blinking hard.

"What time is it?" I ask.

"7:30," she answers. "I have to go to work so you need to get Kyle out of bed and feed him his breakfast."

"Okay." I rub my eyes and sit up. My mouth feels dry and cracked and my head pounds. Hung over. Mom turns and walks away, stopping to turn on the light so I don't just go back to sleep. She turns and looks at me for a second with a funny little smile on her face. She's wearing her pink robe with a pair of purple sweatpants. She has a fuzzy blue slipper on one of her feet; the other is bare. She turns and heads up the stairs and I remember. I can't believe it still slips my mind. My brain still has trouble remembering that my brother is gone. Throughout the day I slide in and out of fleeting moments when I become the person I thought I was before he died. A kid with a shitty family and a shitty job and probably what most people would consider an overall shitty life, but at least it was me. I felt like *me*. It might seem shitty to most people, but I was used to being Jake. Just Jake. I was comfortable with my life and with my family, at least somewhat. It was what I knew and even though we may have been fucked up and dysfunctional, I always sort of thought we worked in some way. Now I'm not so sure.

I hear my mom's footsteps plod up the stairs and the front door opens and slams shut. Her purple clad legs cross in front of the window and she gets into the car, starts it up, and backs out of the driveway. On her way to work. Dressed like a fucking rodeo clown.

I have to do something.

My family was always fucked up. My mom's been a little crazy for pretty much as long as I can remember, but I'm sure she wasn't always that way. She couldn't have been, could she? When I think of my parents meeting and falling in love and getting married, I don't even picture the same people that I know they are. My dad is thinner and has longish hair that he combs in a swoop that hides one of his eyes mysteriously. He's handsome and he smiles devilishly. He stands tall and confident, not like the hunched over, pot-bellied troll he's become. And mom's poodle skirt *swish-swishes* when she walks, rocking her shoulders back and forth, her chin held high like a runway model. I see them meeting and falling in love like movie stars, looking into each other's eyes and knowing immediately that they are under the spell of love, standing in a sparkling spotlight from above, somewhere unseen in the sky, their hair blowing back as they embrace and, in slow motion, my father lifts my mother into the air and swings her around and around, her skirt flowing around her like a ribbon.

I see this memory sometimes and I hold it like an unquestionable truth, but the people I see in my life are not the people I see in my mind. I don't really know if they ever were. But they must have been in love, right? My father must have fallen in love with a beautiful, sane, and proper person. A person capable of functioning normally, of loving, of understanding. I've never known that person, but she must be inside my mother somewhere. They must have been happy and in love once.

I feel suddenly ashamed for staying away from home at a time like this. And for how badly I wanted to hide my family from Jackie. I'm afraid that if she meets my mother, if she finds out about my dad, she will see that we come from two different planets. She will never look at me the same way again. Her eyes will fall on me, sharp and suspicious, like something to be watched, studied. Something not to be trusted.

I can't keep going like this. I can't keep pretending that nothing has happened. My family wasn't exactly The Cleavers to begin with, but whatever we did have is almost completely dissolved now, and I am the only one who can save it. I am the only one who can get any of it back. I don't expect that we'll ever be the perfect family—I'm not an idiot, after all. But I know we can function; in our own way, and as the people we are, we *can* function as a family. We did it before Kyle was born, so why couldn't we do it again?

I know, suddenly and without a doubt, what I must do to help my mother and make us a family again. It seems so simple that I can't believe it took me so long to realize it.

I have to find my father.

I need to tell him about Kyle. Maybe he's heard by now—seen Kyle's picture in the paper or heard his name from a bartender or some other drunk babbling about the dead retard whose family lived at the bottom of the hill, drunkenly unaware that the boy's father downed drinks, hollow-eyed and slurring, only feet away. But I don't know how to find my dad. I don't even really know where to look. The five or six seedy dive bars that dot Browerton's downtown drag would be the obvious place to start, but I'm sixteen. They probably won't even let me in the door. But I have to try. Maybe if I go during the day, when families bring their kids in and give them quarters to play video games while they sip happy hour beers. Even if I don't find him, I could at least ask around. See if anyone knows where he hangs out. I don't know what good finding my dad will do anyway, but maybe I can dry him out long enough for him to talk to my mother. They're practically strangers now, but they must have been in love at some time, right? They must have some kind of connection, deep down, that could surface long enough for them to talk like the civilized people that they must have once been. What would come of it, I don't know. I don't even know if it would do either of them any good. But I do know that it would be the closest I can come to having a family right now. The closest I've come to having a family in a long time. Kyle is gone, gone forever, but if I could get the three of us—me, my mom, and my dad—in one room at the same time, even for a little while, maybe we could be a family again. Maybe Kyle's death doesn't have to be for nothing. Maybe his being gone can bring us back together.

It's a little after noon and, unable to sleep after Mom left for work, I've been up since early this morning. The four Tylenol I swallowed with a glass of orange juice have more or less numbed my headache and I've drank enough water that I can hear it sloshing in my stomach when I walk. So, overall, I feel surprisingly good for how much I drank last night.

Jackie coughs twice and rolls over. Opens her eyes a little and lets out something that's not quite a groan and not quite a sigh.

"Oh my God," she croaks. "I feel like a pile of shit."

"That's weird 'cause I was just going to head upstairs and cook up a pile of shit for breakfast," I joke. "It's sort of my specialty." She doesn't laugh.

"I don't even remember last night," she says. "How did we get here? I assume this is your house?"

"Yup," I say. "We drove here. Or I drove here, I should say. Your car's outside." She closes her eyes and nods gently. Brings her right hand to her face and massages her temples. "Do you have a headache?" I ask. "I could get you an aspirin or something if you think your stomach could handle it."

"It's worth a shot," she says. "I don't know if I could possibly feel much worse." In the bathroom I open the medicine cabinet and can't find any aspirin. I shake three Midol into my hand and fill a cup with tap water.

"These aren't what I was after, but they should do the trick," I tell her. Her hand shakes as I drop the pills into her palm. She takes them one at a time, almost systematically, tipping her head back, tossing a pill to the back of her mouth, then sipping the water. *Plop plop plop.* Like a machine. She holds the water out to me and I tell her to try to keep sipping on it. Her skin looks pale and shiny, like it's stretched too thin. Her eyes look deep and sunken, rimmed with dark circles. Her hair clings to her face in sweaty ringlets.

"Is there anything else I can get you?" I ask. "You don't look so good."

"Gee, thanks." She smiles.

"I didn't mean . . .," I say. "You know what I mean. You look like . . . well, you look like you feel like a pile of shit."

Suddenly her face changes. Her eyes widen and her body tenses up noticeably.

"What?" I ask. "What?"

She answers with one word: "Sick." I run to the bathroom and grab the wicker garbage can, but whoever emptied it last didn't replace the liner. No time to find anything else. I run back to the living room and by the time I reach Jackie she has vomited into her hands. Yellowish fluid seeps between her fingers, dangling toward the ground in thin strands. Her breathing is heavy and manic, punctuated by loud, forceful heaves that she suppresses with obviously painful effort. She looks up at me through a lock of sweaty blonde curls. Even half dead she's fucking beautiful. She opens her mouth to say something, but nothing comes out but a dry heave. I set the wastebasket on the floor in front of her. It barely touches the floor before she picks it up and buries her face inside, vomiting loudly. I don't know what to do. Should I sit next to her and pat her back, let her know that I'm here? Maybe hold her hair back like my mom used to, whispering *Shhhhhh . . . you're going to be fine, just fine.* I've never been good at getting inside people's heads, knowing what they want. Does she need someone to comfort her at a time like this, or is she embarrassed and would rather I went away and didn't see her like this?

Just Jake | 51

She looks up at me pleadingly then vomits again. I mumble something about breakfast and disappear up the stairs.

On my way to the kitchen, I glimpse Kyle's wheelchair in the living room. Normally, Mom or I would push Kyle into the middle of the floor facing the television, so it immediately strikes me as odd that his chair is closer to the wall, facing the piano in the corner of the room. The piano bench has been pulled to the side, Kyle's chair positioned in its place. I approach it slowly, like I'm entering the room of a sleeping child and, standing behind it, I grasp both of the blue rubber handles, tightly lacing my fingers into the grips. The wheels squeak faintly as I wheel the chair backward enough to sit. It feels odd to sit in Kyle's spot. In the seven or eight years that he's had his chair, I've never once sat in it. It feels small and alien to me, yet somehow comfortable. I settle into it, scooting backward and laying my head on the headrest, eyes closed. I try to clear my mind. What was it like to be Kyle? Who was he behind the gurgling, drooling mask? Maybe his mind functioned like mine. Maybe he was as aware as I am of the world he lived in. Maybe life for Kyle was a constant struggle to interact. To communicate with and be a part of the world around him, a world that he saw and heard and felt and understood just as I do. I wonder who I was. To him, I mean. Was I a good brother? Was I a good person? Did I treat him like a brother, or even like a person? Or did my actions suggest that he was nothing more to me than an inanimate fixture in my house? An obstacle to be negotiated and pushed out of the way? An image of Kyle creeps into my mind, and I'm glad to finally be able to picture him as something more than the crumpled, grey picture in my pants pocket. He bucks in his chair, head turning tightly from side to side, as my hands gallop across the keyboard, playing *The William Tell Overture*. In all the hours that Kyle has been in the room with me while I played piano, all of the classics that he has heard from Bach to Handel to Wagner, *The William Tell Overture* was the only one that ever solicited a reaction. I always assumed that he equated it with *The Lone Ranger*, one of his favorite T.V. shows. Although I had learned the entire overture, I only played the finale when Kyle was around—the familiar *da da dum, da da dum, da da dum dum dum* so commonly heard on cartoons and slapstick sitcoms.

My fingers find the keys and start into the first movement of Kyle's song, slowly at first, then faster, my hands sliding over the keys as I close my eyes and tilt my head back. A strange feeling comes over me: a thickness in my limbs, and a deep, electric tingle. A fuzzy grey fog moves in slowly, swallowing me. I feel myself giving in to the feeling, letting myself float. Suddenly, the feeling begins to fade like clouds rolling out after a storm. It's over as quickly as it began.

I open my eyes and Jackie is standing in the doorway, leaning her head and shoulder against the wall, her arms crossed. The corners of her mouth are turned up slightly in a sort of half-grin. Her eyes, still dark and sunken-looking, have in them a lost, faraway look. Her eyes are on me but it's almost like she's not looking *at* me so much as *through* me or *into* me. It sounds dumb, but I swear to God it's true. I stop playing.

"Hey," I say.

"Hey."

"How long you been standing there?"

"For a little while," she says. "That was brilliant. You're talented."

"Ah," I say, waving her compliment off. "I've just been playing for a long time. You could do it too if you'd been playing for as long as I have."

"I doubt it," she says, plopping down on the couch. "How long?"

"Since I was three," I say. "So I guess about thirteen years."

"You mean you started taking lessons when you were three or you just started banging on the keys when you were three?"

"I never took lessons," I say. "I just started playing. It's just sort of something I've always been able to do, I guess." She lays back on the couch and throws an arm over her face to block out the light. "You feeling any better?"

"Not really sure," she says. "I'll live, I think." Not sure what else to say, I ask if she plays any instruments. "No. Not really. I always wanted to play drums. My parents always wanted me to play flute. I guess it fit into their upper class expectation of what a girl should do."

"And?"

"And I was never interested."

"No," I say. "I mean, what about the drums? Did you ever learn to play?"

"Nah," she answers, her face still shielded from sight.

"Why not?" I ask. "Why didn't you just get your dad to buy you a drum set for one of your birthdays or something?"

"Because I just didn't, okay?" she answers, obviously annoyed.

"Think you'd be able to eat?" I ask, changing the subject. "I know it seems like the last thing in the world you'd want to do right now, but trust me: it's probably the only thing that'll make you feel better."

"Mmmmmmmm . . ." she considers. Then, "I'll give it a shot, I guess. There's definitely an unpleasant feeling in my stomach, but I doubt it's hunger." I laugh out loud and she manages a chuckle. "What'd you have in mind?"

"That's up to you," I say. "I'm not as good at cooking as I am at playing piano, but let's just say I've prepared a lot of my own meals."

"Surprise me," she says. "I don't really feel like making any decisions right now. But make something that takes a while; I could use a nap."

"Those pills I gave you were Midol," I say. "They're loaded with caffeine. Sorry."

"Right now I don't think it'll matter," she says. In less than a minute her breathing grows heavy and rhythmic.

In the kitchen, I pull out a large bowl and a whisk. I haven't made them in a long time, but I've got a pretty good recipe for made-from-scratch pancakes. I take my time making them to give Jackie a chance to get some sleep. When I've got a pretty good sized stack ready to go, I wake her up.

"Breakfast," I say, holding the plate of pancakes out to her. She stirs groggily, then: "They smell great." She sits up and I sit next to her, pulling the coffee table, covered in newspaper clippings, food wrappers, and various crumbs and debris, closer to the sofa. I'm embarrassed that she's seeing my house now. Last night when I brought her in she was drunk and the house was shrouded in darkness. Now that's she sobered up and the sun has risen, I'm allowing my eyes to scour every corner of the room. A dirty sock here. A moldy piece of bread there. The light coming in through the window seems to fall on each imperfection, lighting it up like a beacon, revealing to Jackie the truth about me, about the life I live.

We eat together: one plate, two forks. They're not the best batch I've ever made, but they're magic for an empty, hung-over stomach. The room is silent except for the ticking of the wall clock and the sounds of our chewing and swallowing.

"How's it working out for you?" I ask. "The eating, I mean."

"Actually, I feel better already," she says. "I still have a little headache but my stomach is feeling way better. Another hour or two and my brain may actually be capable of simple calculations again."

I like this girl. She's witty.

"What day is it?" she asks.

"Saturday, I think," I say. "Honestly, I'm not really sure. It's summer. The concept of each day having a name doesn't really compute during the summer. It doesn't have to, know what I mean?"

"I guess," she says. "I suppose I should get home. I told my parents I was staying over at Megan's house. Hopefully my mom hasn't called Megan's mom or anything; she does shit like that sometimes. She always worries about me and watches me like I'm a fucking baby. I'm eighteen years old, for God's sake. I don't even know why I still live at home."

"Why do you still live at home?" I ask, hoping I'm not treading on ground I shouldn't. "I mean, you must have graduated high school already, right?"

"Yeah," she says, then pauses like she's not sure what to say next.

"Sorry if it's none of my business," I say. "I was just . . ."

"It's fine, Jake," she says. "Yeah, I graduated last year. From Clouton. That's where my parents live. My dad owns a bank there—I already told you that, I think—and my mom is a nurse at the hospital."

"Oh, really?" I say. "My mom's a nurse too. Or . . . . she used to be." I'm hoping she won't ask why my mom is no longer a nurse, and she doesn't. She sips a little more water and lays her head on the table.

"So," I say, "I'll understand if you don't really feel like talking right now, but I was wondering if you'd tell me about your family."

"Tell you what?" she asks. "My dad owns a bank and my mom's a nurse, like I said."

"I don't know. Tell me *about* them. What are they like? Are they nice? Are they shitty? Do they ignore you? Are they scientologists? Do they walk on their hands? Are they . . ."

"Jeez, Jake," she says. "I get the idea. You're fucking weird." She says it with a smile. "My parents are . . . well, they're pretty much perfect." She glances up at me quickly, then back down at her hands. "I pretty much come from a perfect sitcom family like you see on T.V. My parents are gainfully employed, we live in a nice house—no picket fence, though—I have one older brother and one younger sister, we have an old dog named 'Simon.' I don't know. That's about it, I guess." She glances up at me again and shrugs.

"But what are they like?" I ask, pushing forward. I want to know if her life could possibly be anything like mine. If she could possibly ever understand the kind of world that I've come from, that I still live in. "I mean, what's your family life like? What's it like to . . . I don't know . . . what's it like to be you, I guess?"

"I don't know," she says. "I've never been anyone else, so to me it just seems normal." She sounds like she feels the need to apologize for something. "I don't really know what to say. It's nice, I guess. My parents are a little too protective and controlling sometimes. They still hold onto this image of me as their perfect little princess. Like they'd shit a brick if they thought I was drinking or smoking or anything like that. I swear to God they'd still have me in frilly dresses and pigtails if I'd let them."

"That sucks," I say.

"Yeah," she says. "Pigtails are okay, I guess. I do those sometimes." She smiles for the first time since waking. "I guess it can be a good thing, though, too. The way my parents treat me, I mean. I pretty much get what I want. My parents have money and spending it is the main way they know of to demonstrate their love, I guess."

"Hence the asking for a car for your birthday," I say.

Just Jake | 55

"Exactly," she says, and smiles.

"What else?"

"I don't know," she says. She squints her eyes and scratches behind her right ear. "Like I said, my parents are straight out of a sitcom. My mom drives a minivan with an "Abortion Kills" bumper sticker in the back window. My dad is a church elder who wears a suit and golfs a lot. We go on family vacations every year. We own a cute little cabin on a lake. All that shit." I picture her spending her summers at a lake cabin, swimming and jet-skiing and fishing. Sunbathing. "I really don't see why you're so interested in my family, Jake. There's really nothing too interesting to know."

"To me it's interesting," I say.

"Why?" she asks. "What's your family like?"

"I don't know," I say, wondering how much I should reveal. Do I lie to her? Do I tell her the truth, just spill it all out on the table? Do I avoid the issue altogether? "They're different. Different from yours anyway, I guess."

"Different how?" She smiles and her eyes light up a little.

"Not like a sitcom, that's for sure. Maybe *Married with Children* or something like that." She laughs a little—just what I was hoping for. "You should probably get home though, huh?" I say. "Do you feel well enough to drive yet?" I ask.

"Well, it doesn't sound like the most fun thing in the world right now," she says. "But I should probably go."

"If you need to stay here a little longer you can," I say. "Sleep a little more or whatever. But I can drive us as far as the store if you're ready to go."

"Sounds good," she says, wincing as she picks herself up off the couch. "Let's do this. I'll slam an orange juice or something when we get there and I should be all right to drive home."

"Sure," I say. "Want a glass of water for the road?" I fill up a glass with ice and water and hand it to her.

Outside, I open Jackie's car door for her before getting in myself. I turn the ignition and it sputters. I turn it again and it just clicks.

"Try it again," she says. "It does that sometimes."

I turn it again and it starts. Jackie reminds me to put my seatbelt on before I back out of the driveway. The inside of the car is hot and stuffy. The backs of my arms stick to the beige nylon seats. Jackie digs a pair of sunglasses out of the glove box and sips unsteadily on the glass of water. I roll down my window. She leaves hers up. The day is hot and bright, the air thick and wet. Ripples of heat rise from the black pavement as I creep Jackie's car toward downtown Browerton and the Quikmart, hoping not to hit any bumps or take any quick turns that might agitate her headache or worse. The last thing she needs is to explain vomit-stained car seats to her Donna Reed parents. We drive in silence, Jackie slinked low in her seat and me shielding my eyes from the sun. Twice I instinctively reach for the radio knob to kill the silence, both times remembering Jackie's hangover.

On Main Street, we roll past the four-block strip that contains the majority of the local bars (full-time hangouts for Browerton's best and brightest) and I picture my father sitting inside one of them with a cigarette hanging out the corner of his mouth and a half-full mug of cheap tap beer in his hand. I have to find him. I have to do it tonight. I don't know where my mother is and I don't know how much time she has left or if it's too late for her already. Against what would normally qualify as my better judgment, I decide to speak without thinking because I know that thinking usually only serves to make me chicken out.

"Are you going to be in trouble when you get home?" I ask, turning to look at Jackie, who startles from a half-sleep.

"Hmm?"

"I was just wondering if you're going to be in trouble or anything when you get home."

"I don't think so," she says, scooting up in her seat. "I told my parents I was staying at Megan's, remember? I don't see any reason why they'll suspect anything."

"So do you think you'll be able to do anything outside the house tonight?"

"Jake, I'm eighteen," she says.

"Sorry. I guess what I meant is, would you want to do anything tonight? Like, with me?" I'm gripping the steering wheel a little tighter than usual, but overall I'm not as nervous as I should be. I'm comfortable with this girl. She makes me happy. On some level I think I make sense to her. Or at least parts of me do.

"Maybe," she says, trying not to smile. "What'd you have in mind?"

"Actually, I kind of wanted to go to Sammy's."

"Who's Sammy?"

"No," I say. "I mean the bar Sammy's. We just drove past it."

"You want to go to a bar?" she asks, turning to face me in her seat. "I just said I'm only eighteen, Jake. And you're, what, sixteen? Seventeen?"

"Seventeen in a few months," I say. "I don't think it'll matter, though. We're not going to drink or anything."

"Then why go?" she asks. "I don't get it."

"I need to find someone. My dad actually. I need to find my dad."

"What do you mean 'find' your dad?" she asks, her voice raising slightly. "Did you lose him?"

"Sort of," I say, taking a deep breath. "I don't really see him that often."

"Oh," she says. "I'm sorry. I didn't mean to bring up . . . I mean, I didn't know your parents were separated."

"They're not," I say. "It's just . . . I don't really know how to explain it exactly. My dad just doesn't come home much."

"I don't get it," she says.

"I don't get it either, really," I say. "He used to be around all the time, like a regular dad or whatever. He started drinking a lot and then he pretty much just quit coming home. I mean, he comes home once in a while, but he's always piss drunk and he pretty much just falls into bed or on the couch or whatever and sleeps until he's physically able to get up and start drinking again."

I slow the car down and make the turn into the Quikmart parking lot. My shitty car sits like a sick toad behind the building, right where I left it. I pull into the space next to it.

"You want me to run in and get you something to drink?" I ask. "I can probably get a deal if someone I know is working. And if my boss isn't here."

"I'll go in with you," she says. "It's too damn hot in this car, anyway." The door locks click and I open my door to step out. "Shit!" Jackie yells suddenly and ducks low in her seat. "Get down!" I duck as low as my lanky frame allows in a sardine can sports car and my neck begins to cramp almost immediately.

"Why are we hiding?" I ask, unsure why I'm whispering.

"That lady knows my mom."

"What lady?"

"A lady I just saw in the parking lot," she says. "My mom and her work together." Craning my neck slightly, I'm just barely able to see a tired-looking woman in a lavender sweat suit walking past the rear of the car. She wears thick glasses and a disheveled pseudo-beehive hairdo. She gets into a rusty sedan a few rows back and pulls out of the parking lot.

"She's gone," I say. Jackie inches herself upright and peers cautiously through the rear window.

"You sure?" she asks.

"Yeah," I say. "I saw her get in her car and leave."

"That was close," she says. "I'd be in a shitload of trouble if she saw me and this got back to my mom."

"If what got back to your mom?" I ask.

"You know . . . if my parents found out that I was hung over and hanging out with some guy they've never met instead of spending the night at Megan's like I was supposed to be."

"Oh, yeah. I keep forgetting about the Megan thing," I say. "So that lady was a friend of your mom's?"

"I don't know if they're really friends," she says, stepping out of the car. I get out too and we walk across the parking lot toward the Quikmart. "They work together at the clinic in Clouton."

"Hard to believe that lady's a nurse," I say. "She looked like a freakin' bag lady. Like she puts her makeup on with her eyes closed or something."

"Ha ha," Jackie says. "I never said she's a nurse. I just said she works with my mom."

"Did you see that sweat suit she was wearing?" I ask. "Horrible. She looked like . . ."

"Alright, alright," she says. "I get the idea, Jake. Can you shut up for a minute? You're not exactly making my headache any better." We enter the store in silence. I'm a little scared to talk because I feel like I pissed Jackie off or something. I never know what to do in these situations. When somebody asks me to shut up like that, I usually end up just shutting up. Some people might start apologizing or asking what they did wrong or whatever, but I just keep my mouth shut. Whatever it was she'll forget it in a little while anyway. I hope.

This jerk named Brad or Blake or something is working the till. A real "Mr. Personality" if ever there was one. We each get an orange juice and I get a stick of beef jerky.

"Hey, Jake!" he says, all excited like we're best buddies or something. "Not working today, huh?" I almost comment about his brilliant deduction but decide it's probably better if I just keep my mouth shut. I roll my eyes hard and walk out.

We're crossing the pavement outside and Jackie seems relaxed again. She's chugged half of her orange juice and I'm wondering if her headache is starting to go away.

"So what do you think about tonight?" I ask. "Looking for my dad, I mean?"

"Honestly, Jake," she says, "I think it sounds like a blast." She opens her car door, settles into the seat, and zooms off. Just before she turns out of the parking lot she rolls her window down, extends her hand and gives me a little wave. I've got that weird, floaty feeling again. This girl has got to be a dream.

I stand in the parking lot and let the sun beat down on me for awhile. It's a really hot day; probably at least in the eighties. I take a drink of the orange juice and feel the cold tingle as it rolls down my throat and settles in my stomach.

My shitty car has left a sizeable oil stain in the parking lot. Absently, I reach into my pocket for the keys.

Which I don't have.

Shit.

Jackie took my keys last night before we left. I wipe beads of sweat from my neck and start walking.

Chapter 10

It's after 3:00 by the time I get home and Mom's not back yet. I'm starting to worry about her. It's not like they would have let her work like that. Maybe on Halloween or something, but it's the middle of freaking August. You'd think they would have just sent her home. I wish she had a cell phone or something so I could get a hold of her, but she'd sooner have a sex change than actually enter the 21st century. Techno-logically, anyway. Hell, the phone in her room is one of those old rotary things. It's khaki-colored and about the size of a Volkswagen. You know the kind; you've probably seen them on old sitcoms, sitting on the nightstand between the separate beds that the Moms and Dads conspicuously do not share.

Mom doesn't really have any friends I can check with either. I guess there's Helen, Kyle's old babysitter, but I doubt Mom's been in contact with anyone lately. Lots of people have been calling the house with their condolences and all but she hasn't been answering the phone. Aren't people supposed to drop by the house with Jell-O molds and hotdish and shit after someone dies? Isn't that how it works? Come to think of it, maybe they have been. I guess I haven't been home as much lately as I should. But I'm going to make up for all that. Tonight Jackie and I are going to find my dad and bring him home and by that time Mom will be here and we'll sit down together and remember Kyle and talk about him and deal with all of this. And we'll be fine. We'll be together as a family and we'll be fine.

I wonder where we'll find my dad. He'll be out and he'll be drunk; of that there's little doubt. How will he react when he sees me? I don't even remember the last time we actually sat down and talked. Usually we nod to each other at the very most, and more often than not I just see him passed out on the couch on my way to work or whatever and not a word is said between us. I also wonder when would be the best time to go. I don't know if there's any chance at all of catching the guy even half-way sober, but that would be ideal. For all I know he's downing gin and tonics by noon every day. Wouldn't surprise me one bit. I imagine his days are the same when he wakes up at some floozy's house as when he wakes up here. He must have a girlfriend or something 'cause he sure as hell doesn't seem to need our roof over his head too often. I've heard Mom mention a few times that she's pretty sure he's got some girlfriend down the road in Clouton. Knowing my dad, though, he probably just heads out to the bar and finds himself a different bar whore every night. He's not the most educated or cultured guy in the world, but he can be pretty damn smooth when he wants to be. Especially when it'll keep him from having to crash here with us.

I doubt it'll do any good, but maybe I should give Helen a call just in case she has heard from Mom. I'm not crazy about talking to adults on the phone, especially attention-starved old ladies who can't seem to get it through their head that I'm sixteen, not six, but I don't know what else to do.

I dial the phone. Three rings in and I'm relieved that I'll probably just have to leave a message, but then she picks up.

"Hello?" Perky as hell.

"Hi, Helen?"

"This is she." *She,* not her. "Who's calling?"

"It's Jake. Jake Withers." I really do not want to have this conversation.

"Oh, Jake." Her voice changes immediately from *I'm talking to a human being* to *I'm talking to a poor, lost puppy that has been kicked repeatedly.* "How are you, honey? Hangin' in there?"

"Yeah, I guess," I say, trying to speed this along. "Have you talked to my mom today at all?"

"Patty? Why no, Jake. No, I haven't," she says. "How is your mother? She hasn't answered my calls the last few days. I sure hope the two of you are doing okay." She pauses. Starts to say something then stops herself. I'm not sure what to say.

The door is open.

Helen may be a smothering, annoyingly over-protective old woman, but that may be just what I need right now. I could tell her about Mom. Tell her that Mom has gone off the deep end again, and probably all the way off this time. Maybe Helen would know what to do, who to talk to. But I don't want to get all kinds of cops and therapists and shit involved. I'd like to stay as far away from those people as I can. And besides, when I bring Dad back tonight and sober him up we're all going to work this out tomorrow. They'll both realize how fucked up they've been for years and they'll patch all of this up. Kyle died, for God's sake. That's got to get their attention. That's got to be the wake-up call they need.

"Jake, are you there?" Her voice has gone up a full octave; all the way to desperately concerned old lady range.

"Yeah, I'm here," I say. "We're good. I mean, you know, not good. But we're okay. I was just wondering if you'd seen Ma. I thought she'd be home from work by now, but I'm sure she'll be here any minute."

"Are you sure, Jake? I could come by. Do you need anything?"

"No, Helen," I say. "Really. We're okay. Ma and I are getting by okay." I don't mention Dad. Helen has made sure not to ask. Not real surprising.

"Well, I'll see you Monday afternoon, Jake, okay?" she says. "If not sooner. It'll be a beautiful service, Jake. I just know it. It will be absolutely beautiful. A real celebration of life. You know everyone at church really loved that little brother of yours. He was a ray of sunshine. Always. He really was and we all knew it. He's up there with God right now flying around with his little wings and I'll bet he's just tickled pink, Jake."

Shit.

The funeral.

I completely fucking forgot about the funeral.

"Yeah," I say. "See you then. I gotta go. I think Ma just pulled into the driveway."

"Well, you tell Patty I said 'hello' and that if she needs anything, anything at all . . ."

Click. Sorry, Helen, but I've listened to about all I can handle.

My brother's funeral is Monday. Today is . . . what? Saturday? Less than 48 hours away and I didn't even remember. How's Ma gonna handle this? Will she go? Should I try to make her? I'm too young for his shit. I'm sixteen years old, for God's sake. I shouldn't be taking care of my mother, trying to decide whether she's in any shape to attend her son's funeral. Shouldn't *she* be holding *me* right now? Telling me everything's going to be okay? Isn't that what mothers do? Aren't parents supposed to be some all-knowing foundation that you can always stand on and count on? I wish I had Jackie's family. If Jackie's little brother died, her parents would know what to do. They would say, "I realize this is a hard time for you, Jake. It's a hard time for all of us. Go ahead and take some time off work. You deserve it. This isn't easy for anyone to go through, especially at your age. We love you, Jake, and we're here for you. Your family is here for you if you need anything. Anything at all." That's what a fucking family is supposed to be. A support group or something. People who understand you that you can talk to when you need someone. Sometimes I think I'd prefer to have an abusive family or something. At least they'd have to be home to yell at me or kick my ass or whatever. At least they'd have to be present. My dad is so drunk he doesn't even know he has a fucking family and my mom is as retarded as Kyle is. Was. I swear to God.

Dammit. Where's Jackie? She has my keys and I don't even have her fucking number and I need my car to find my fucking dad and she said she would come with me. She lives in fucking Clouton and I don't have my keys and I can't drive my car there to get my keys because I need my keys to start my fucking car and what the hell am I supposed to do? Where's my mom? Where's my fucking dad? I need my keys, my damn car keys. I need a nap.

Chapter 11

I'm swimming around that staircase again. That weird underground staircase and the birds are flying overhead. Their shadows swim across the staircase like fish climbing out of the water, then back in, then out again. Everything seems real serene but I can't stop thrashing through the water because I know I'm alone. Jackie's not here this time. Then, from above the water, a shadow cuts the sun and I can see the top of the staircase. My eyes strain to adjust, to see through the murky water. The sun disappears behind the shadow again and I see. My father stands on a small landing at the top of the staircase. He doesn't move and he can't see me. I struggle to swim to the staircase but I can only thrash aimlessly, turning around and around in the dark water. The birds swoop and dart overhead, their shadows refracted on each step that I can't reach.

I wake up on the couch and I'm happy to leave the dream this time. The clock on the VCR says it's 6:33. Missed *Jeopardy* again, but I suppose that's the least of my concerns. I call out for Mom just in case she came home while I was asleep but there's no answer. Where the hell is she? And where the hell is Jackie? I guess I've started to take for granted that she sort of just shows up when I need her like some kind of fairy Godmother. Well, I need her now. I need my fucking car keys.

I go to the kitchen and throw together a sandwich from some crap I find in the fridge and grab a half-full bag of potato chips from the cupboard. Back in the living room I click the TV on and eat. *Wheel of Fortune*'s on. That'll do, I guess. I like *Wheel of Fortune* okay. I see the headlights of a car turning onto our street, but they come and go without slowing down. Could have been Mom. Could have been Jackie. No luck. I'm starting to hope that I'll not only be able to get into a bar long enough to find my dad, but maybe some dumb bartender will even give me a couple drinks. I guess, in a way, I sort of look old for my age. I'm taller than most kids, and I sort of have facial hair—a blondish-red five o' clock shadow of a beard that may or may not show up by the glow of neon beer signs.

By the time I reach Main Street the sun has pretty much set and it's cooled off a lot. Actually, I kinda wish I'd brought a hoodie. Man, walking is nice sometimes. It's like you don't really realize how beautiful your town is until you walk around it a little. Browerton is kind of a picturesque place when you get a chance to see it a little better. Funny the things you notice on foot that you'd never see in a car. A little shoestore, shrouded in shadows, is nestled kitty-corner a ways back from the sidewalk. It's surrounded by overgrown weeds and a hand-painted Red Wings Boots sign hangs above the door. I guess it's possible that I haven't noticed it because the place isn't open anymore, but it strikes me as weird. Out of place.

I'm half-hoping to see Jackie drive by, scouring the streets looking for me, or maybe on her way to Sammy's to meet me. She definitely has a knack for just sort of showing up. And, truth be told, now that I'm just a few blocks away, I'm getting pretty nervous about walking into the bar looking for my dad. I imagine I'd feel a little better if I had somebody with me. Jackie, especially. Something tells me a scrawny, sixteen-year-old kid will get kicked out of a bar faster than a scrawny, sixteen-year-old kid and an attractive eighteen-year-old girl. Hell, *woman.*

There's a small group of baby boomers standing outside Sammy's smoking cigarettes and talking way too loud. I keep walking. I'll come around the block or something and then go in. I don't want anyone standing outside when I go in. I might be able to pull off looking twenty-one in the low light of a bar; outside on a sunny summer evening is a whole different story. Hopefully I can get in and make my way to a dark corner table before anyone gets a real good look at me. Assuming Sammy's has dark corner tables; I've never actually been inside.

When I come around the block there's no one outside. The sidewalk is littered with flattened cigarette butts and a cloud of bugs crowds around the light over the door. I pull my hat down low and stick my hands in my pockets. Pull them out. Stick them back in again. My right hand touches a crumpled piece of paper: Kyle. I want to take his picture out and look at it. Remind myself why I'm here, why I'm doing this. But I don't.

The inside of the bar is small, smaller than it looks from outside, and there's a sour smell in the air. It's not exactly vomit, but it's not exactly *not* vomit, either. I'm hoping it's one of those smells that your nose stops noticing after a while, because if it isn't I don't know how long I'm going to be able to sit in this joint.

66 | Erik P. Block

The bar is off to my right. It's small—only five or six stools line the front of it, with three or four more along one side. The stools are empty except for an older woman with dyed red hair and way too much makeup sitting in front of some sort of poker machine or something at the end of the bar. She's got this horrible flowery dress on. I always figured Mimi or whatever her name is from Drew Carey was an exaggeration but this lady convinces me otherwise.

I don't see a bartender. Four guys huddle around a pool table to my left. The kind of guys who have their names sewn on the pockets of their work shirts, which they don't bother changing out of before coming to the bar. I suppose in a place like this, those shirts are like some kind of badge of honor. Like, "Hey, look at me! I bet I put in more hours at my shitty, manual labor job than you do!" Three are middle-aged men, hairy and pot-bellied; the fourth is younger. I recognize the younger guy from somewhere but I can't remember where. All four glance up at me when I walk in but don't seem to think I'm worth their attention. So far, so good. There's a small stage in the back left corner, and a few feet to the right of it, two electronic dart machines. No one is playing. There's maybe ten people in the whole bar and none of them's my dad.

Suddenly I'm not sure if grabbing a table in a dark corner is the best idea. With so few people in here, maybe that would look too obvious. Should I sit at the bar? Just sidle on up like I own the place and order a drink? Somehow I'm afraid that my version of acting like I own the place looks suspiciously like a nervous, dorky, underage kid trying to act like he owns the place. But I don't see a bartender around right now and what's the worst they can do to me, anyhow? Kick me out? My dad's not here anyway, so I guess I've answered the question I came to answer, for that matter. But he could show up. I'd be surprised if he didn't show up, actually. There are other bars in Browerton that I could check, but everyone in town knows that Sammy's is where the drunk old guys go. Don't get me wrong: I imagine every small town bar has their regular crew of drunk old guys, but in Browerton, Sammy's is where it's at for the old hookup scene, if you can imagine there is such a thing. Every story I've heard about marital infidelity in Browerton has started at Sammy's.

I take a deep breath and sit at the stool closest to the edge of the bar; just two seats separate me and the makeup lady. The bar is almost dead quiet except for the sound of the lady's long, red fingernails tapping the machine's screen, which gets obnoxious quick. I slide my stool forward a little and rest my elbows on the bar, trying to look relaxed. From behind me comes a loud *crack* as one of the grizzly men makes a break shot. The jukebox clicks audibly and begins to play. I'm relieved that the silence is broken, even if it is Garth Brooks or Tim McGraw or whoever crooning about losing his wife. The younger guy over at the pool table starts singing along. Badly.

The makeup lady curses not quite under her breath, looks up from the poker machine and picks up her nearly empty drink. I'm trying to appear fascinated by the bar's wood grain while I watch her out of the corner of my eye. The music helps things a little, but I still feel like a kid trying to be a man, which I guess I am.

"Hi," I hear the makeup lady say. I look up, hoping she's not talking to me. She's waving and a flap of fat jiggles on the back of her arm. I sort of look over my shoulder to make sure no one just came in the door. She's talking to me, all right.

"Hey," I say, a little quieter than I'd like.

"Help you, dear?" she asks, tilting her head to the side like a dog.

"I . . . don't know." *Help me? What the hell is she talking about?*

"You don't know?" She smiles like a cartoon and starts to get up from her chair. "Well if you don't know, who does?"

"I don't know," I say again, like a fucking broken record. *Say something, Jake. You sound suspiciously like a high-school kid who just snuck into a bar.*

The makeup lady picks up her empty glass and walks around to the back of the bar. "Mugs'r on special tonight. Buck seventy-five 'til eleven, then it's back up to full price." *She's the bartender. I'm an idiot. Order something quick, Jake, before she asks to see your I.D.*

"Actually, a beer sounds good," I say. "Sounds great, really. I'll, uh, I'll have one of those." I point to the biggest, gaudiest looking tap. I don't know shit about different kinds of beer. Most of my beer experience involves either 30-packs or brown-bagged forties. That and whatever my dad would have on hand in the fridge, which was never exactly the good stuff. Whatever that is.

She grabs a big, frosty-looking mug and pours me a beer.

"You in town on business?" she asks, and she winks.

"No, actually," I start and she has to know I'm fidgeting.

"Yeah, you are, dear," she says, and winks again. "You're in town on business."

"Okay," I stammer, not sure what else to say. I take a sip from the beer. It's cold and tastes great. People always say that beer is an acquired taste but I loved it the first time I took a sip. I must've been only about twelve or something and I thought it was great. Which is rare, I guess. So I don't open my mouth and say something dumb, I tip the mug back and drink deeply. I swallow five or six times—big, deep, manly swallows. I'm hoping chugging beer will make her think I'm older, an experienced drinker. But maybe that's a high school thing? I lower the mug and wipe my mouth. I expect the Mimi lady to be standing in front of me, waiting for some sort of explanation of who I am, but she's a ways down the bar already wiping glasses. A belch churns in my stomach, and I let it out as quietly as possible between pursed lips. Half my beer is gone already and that familiar warmth sinks in, starting in my stomach and trickling slowly outward.

I finish my beer and order another. The bartender lady brings me another and goes back to wiping glasses. I'd like to ask her if she knows my dad, maybe knows if he'll be here later or where he is, but I don't really want to advertise my age, even if she does already know. For now, I'm content to drink and hope Dad shows up. I might as well enjoy this while I can, right? And what about Jackie? Where the hell is she? She said she would come with me tonight to do this. This clown behind the bar could have told us we're a married couple on vacation or something. I finish my second beer and I'm barely nervous anymore. I'm slumped back in my chair and I feel like I belong here. I don't know if that's good or bad. My stool squeaks a little as I turn to watch the fat pool-player guys. The younger one is still singing along with the jukebox in a quivering bass.

"'Nother beer?"

I spin my stool to the front and the bartender is right in front of me, leaning onto the bar. Her freckled cleavage bulges from the neck of her dress and I hope noticing doesn't mean I was looking too long.

"Or can I get ya somethin' else?"

"Uh." In an attempt to sound older and more worldly, I decide to change up my order a little. "Actually, I'll take a scotch."

"Straight up?"

"Sure," I say. "Fine."

"Ya sure ya don't need a splash of water in there?"

"Sure," I say. "Water's fine. Ice too."

"On the rocks, it is," she says.

I'm a fucking moron.

The Mimi lady grabs a bottle and a small glass from below the bar. Makes my drink.

"I'm Rosy," she says, setting the drink in front of me.

"Doug," I say, without missing a beat.

"And what kind of business you on, Doug?" she asks. "Browerton don't really have a lot of business needs doin'."

"I . . . am a farmer," I say, and take a sip of my scotch. I'm hoping I've said enough to end the matter. I'm also hoping my mesh trucker's cap is enough to make me look the part, 'cause my baggy jeans, Bad Religion t-shirt and Chuck Taylors sure aren't gonna help any.

"Kinda farmin'?"

Just Jake | 69

"A few kinds," I say. "I got corn, soybeans. That kinda stuff." I peek at her while I take another drink. "I'd rather not talk about work, actually. What's the use in coming to the pub if not to get away from the grind, right?" I peak at her again and she smiles. She must not have noticed that I said "pub." What kind of farmer says "pub?" No kind is my guess.

"Works for me," she says. "Honestly, I don't blame ya. I don't like to talk about my job when I'm here either." She turns away and walks down the bar, cackling like she just made the funniest joke she's heard in years. I take a big swallow of my scotch. I am getting wasted. And I have to piss. I don't see a restroom sign anywhere, but I don't imagine they could be too hard to find in a place like this. A bulletin board hangs on the wall in a little alcove next to the dart machines. You know the kind: flyers for wild game feeds and lawnmowing services and somebody's slutty little daughter who wants to babysit your kids. Those bulletin boards are always next to the bathrooms.

The inside of the john is about the size of a bathtub and smells like shit. And I don't mean that as a euphemism. It actually *smells* like *shit*. The walls are green, wet-looking brick and the only light comes from a bare, smoky-looking bulb above the mirror. I piss and wash my hands. A skinny, awkward, very drunk kid stares back at me from the mirror. I flick off the light and stumble back toward my drink.

The front door opens, and a shaft of sunlight pours into the bar. Through the flood of light, I can just make out a silhouette in the doorway and, though the light has blinded me, I'm struck with the sudden assurance that it's my dad. A jolt hits my body and, involuntarily, I draw a quick, shallow breath. Panicked, I duck back into the shadow of the alcove, just outside the bathroom door. I need to see my father, of course, to get all this shit over with—mom, Kyle's funeral, everything. But I'm suddenly nervous, like I'm about to talk to someone I've never met. In a way, that's not far from true.

The door closes and my eyes adjust. Standing midway between the front door and the pool table are Jackie and the younger pool player that I swear to God I know from somewhere. Jackie's wearing a simple turquoise dress and her hair is pulled up. Almost like some kind of prom 'do. She wears black high-heels and sparkly earrings dangle from her ears. She looks much older than her eighteen years: a refined, even dainty, woman. She smiles, touches the back of her neck, and leans in to hug the guy. Her smile is half-real at best, but she relaxes into the hug. Holds onto the guy for quite a while, squeezing tightly. Definitely not the stiff-bodied, torsos-held-six-inches-apart hug shared between strangers and casual acquaintances. She starts out with her eyes closed, but opens them a few seconds into the hug and scans the room, left to right, right to left. Looking for me. They pull away after what seems like too long and Jackie's hands linger on his forearms a moment longer. The guy shifts his weight to one leg and hooks a thumb in his pocket. Adjusts his blue baseball cap, pulling it off his head, then pulling it on again.

The tech-schooler. It's him; the toady football player. The one I saw with Darrell the other day. He's dressed a little nicer—a little older, I guess you could say—but it's definitely him. He's wearing the same sweaty baseball cap.

Wonder how he knows Jackie? He could be from Clouton, I guess. Could have graduated with her or something, but there's no way the guy's only eighteen. He looks more like twenty-two, twenty-three. And he's hanging out with a bunch of forty-something factory-types. He's *gotta* be a tech-schooler. Diesel Mechanics major is my guess. Plumbing, maybe. But how would he know Jackie then? Unless she went to the tech or something. For how much she knows about me already, I sure don't know much about her. I'm doing my best to hear what they're saying without getting myself noticed. I can hear their voices, but only in murmurs. Can't make out any words.

One of the older guys yells for Toady, trying to get him to come take his turn. Without turning around, he gives them the arm extended, index finger up, international sign for "just a sec." Talks with Jackie for a few more seconds, then goes to take his turn. Jackie looks around the bar again. Checks her watch. It must be around 10:30, 11:00 by now. She walks to the bar—surprisingly graceful considering the high heels—and settles into the stool I was just in. Probably still warm.

I take a deep breath and head back toward the bar. I lock a grin on my face and try to seem casual. When I'm just a few feet away, I hear the bartender ask to see Jackie's I.D.

"She's with me," I tell the bartender, sliding onto the stool next to Jackie. "She's . . . my wife." Jackie turns and looks at me like I have a horn growing out of the middle of my face, but she keeps her mouth shut, goes along with it.

"Well, I apologize, ma'am," says Rosy. "I didn't realize you were Mrs. Doug. Mrs. Doug the corn and soybean farmer." She winks at me again, hard and obvious, and picks up Jackie's cash. "Keep it!" Jackie shouts as Rosy walks away, chuckling.

Jackie turns to me and mouths the words, *What the?* I just shrug.

"I didn't know you were here," Jackie says. "I mean, I was hoping you were. That's why I came, obviously. I just didn't know if you'd be here *now.*"

"Yeah," I say. "I been here a while. Two or three drinks worth at least. Maybe four. Can't remember. Pretty drunk already." I pick up my drink from the bar.

"Well, wait up, will you?" she says and her eyes literally twinkle. "I got some catching up to do." She takes the drink—pinkish, with a slice of lime—to her mouth and drinks from the straw, her cheeks pulled in like a little kid doing a fish impression. She downs an impressive amount in one go, over half the drink. "Your dad?" she asks, eyebrows raised.

"Shhh!" I tilt my head and jab it sideways, indicating the bartender.

"Oh!" she says, and shrugs her shoulders to her ears. Looks at my drink, then back up at me. "I don't . . ."

"Wanna grab a table?" I interrupt. "Over in the corner?"

"Yeah, sure," she says, picking up her drink to follow me.

"Not leaving, are you?" asks Toady, who seems to have snuck up when I wasn't looking.

"No," answers Jackie. "We're just getting a table. Back there." She points with her drink. "Jake, this is Ashlee." He extends his hand and I try not to laugh as I shake it. "Ashlee, this is my friend Jake." *Ashlee? Who the hell names their son Ashlee? No wonder he turned into a muscle-head football player. Probably had to start lifting weights when he was five to keep from getting his ass kicked on the playground everyday. And why am I left guessing his status while I fell victim to the "friend" tag? Just who the hell is this guy?*

I want to put my arm out prom-style and walk Jackie to the back of the bar, away from this Neanderthal, but something stops me—most likely the fact that I'm a gigantic pussy. She looks nervous, like she doesn't know which one of us to talk to, like she owes something to both of us. Toady looks smug, sure of himself. Compared to me, though, pretty much everyone looks that way. The three of us stand silent for a few seconds.

"Anyway, wanna head back and sit down?" I blurt at Jackie, making sure that I look at her and only at her. I don't need Ashlee butting in.

"Sure," she says, looking nervously from Ashlee to me and back. I shuffle backward a few steps, waiting for Jackie to follow. The Neanderthal speaks.

"We actually just finished our game," he says, hooking a thumb back toward the pool table. "Mind if I join you?" *For fuck's sake. I came here to find my dad and now I'm going to be stuck at a table with the girl of my dreams and this obviously enamored ape. He better be well-trained enough to keep his fucking hands to himself.*

I walk back to the table a little ahead of Jackie and Ashlee, making sure to keep my eyes on my feet. I'm trying to look smooth and easygoing, which I imagine I do, considering how drunk I've gotten. I'm trying not to look like an uptight, jealous asshole. I have to remind myself that Jackie's not even my girlfriend. We haven't even kissed. We approach a small booth near the back corner of the bar and I slide in with my back to the restrooms so I can see in case my dad comes in. I slide all the way to the wall to leave room for Jackie. A knot ties itself in my chest as she slides in across from me and Ashlee sits down next to her. *What the fuck?* I can hear blood rushing through my ears and feel my face heating up as Ashlee (fucking *girl's* name) throws an arm up over the booth, behind Jackie's neck. They're both talking and laughing and I can't even hear what they're saying, like their mouths are moving silently. My leg starts to shake and I want to smash my glass over his fucking face, feel the sharp-edged shards slicing through his skin, watch his body slump to the ground in a pool of black blood.

"Jake?"

It's Jackie. I snap out of it.

"You okay, Jake?"

"Yeah," I say. "Yeah, I'm fine. Sorry. I was just . . . ah . . . zoning out, I guess. Pretty drunk."

"Ashlee asked you a question," she says.

"Oh. Sorry, *Ash*lee." I pronounce his name like a disease, spit it through my teeth.

"I was just wondering if you went to the tech." He pulls his hat off and smooths down his hair. Puts it back on. He's balding.

"Ah, no," I say. "I actually . . ." *Shit. Do I tell him I'm in high school? I don't want him to think Jackie's a loser for hanging out with some high school kid. For that matter, I don't want him to think* I'm *a loser because I'm in* high school. *He must know Jackie's not old enough to be in here, so maybe I don't have to worry about that? In case the bartender is his fucking aunt or something?* "I actually don't go to the tech, no," I finish, hoping it will be enough. Ashlee nods and turns back to Jackie. Obviously, he doesn't really care what the hell I do; he just wanted to look like he cared in front of Jackie.

They chat for a few minutes, pretty much ignoring me, before one of Ashlee's friends yells to him that they're taking off. Ashlee leans over in the booth and gives Jackie a hug, then nods to me and smirks a little before standing up and leaving with his friends. *Good fucking riddance.* I want to ask Jackie who he is, how she knows him, but as usual I wimp out. I've never been any good at bringing up issues that are hard to talk about. I guess I'm what you could call a pretender. If I don't know the truth, it can't hurt me, so I pretty much keep myself from knowing the truth.

My eyes are half-closed and my head is lolling like my neck is too weak to hold it up, when Rosy approaches the table.

"I was gonna ask if you two needed another drink," she says, "but I'm thinkin' that might not be such a good idea, eh?" I look over at Jackie and, although she does seem a little drunk, she's nowhere near as bad as I am.

Just Jake | 73

"Actually, I wouldn't mind another Cape Cod," Jackie says. She slams the rest of her drink and slides the glass to the edge of the table.

"Will do, ma'am," Rosy says. "You doin' okay, Doug? Can I get you a water or something? Maybe a cot?"

"Ugghhhhh," I grunt. "Maybe a cot?" I am *dah-runk*, repeating after Rosy like a fucking parrot. My mind is *gone*. "How come you're letting me drink?" I slur. "I'm not even old enough. You know . . ."

"Whaddya mean, Doug?" she says. "A guy like you? Successful farmer and everything? *Gotta* be at least twenty-one, right?" I hear a wink in her voice but I can't actually *see* if she winks or not. Too blurry. Then, a hand on my shoulder, gently inching me over in my seat. Next thing I know, Rosy is sitting next to me, patting me on the head like I'm a dog. A really fucking drunk dog. "I'm no dummy, Jake." The sound of my name coming out of her mouth wakes me up a little. I sit up straight—well, sort of straight—and she has as close to my full attention as I can give. "I know who you are, Jake. Recognized you the second you walked in here—before you even sat down. Your daddy's an old friend of mine. Hell, we went to high school together. He was a year or two younger, of course, but he never had trouble gettin' attention from the ladies. Even the older ones." Rosy leans back and sighs loudly. "Yup, your daddy always was a lady's man. Used to come in here quite a bit. Actually, I used to worry about you a little, Jake. You and that little brother of yours. I'm so sorry to hear about him, by the way." Jackie is leaning forward, fascinated, glued to the edge or her seat like she's watching a really good movie. Even in the low light of Sammy's Lounge, I can see that her eyes are shiny, moist. I feel a weight in my own heart, but not for Kyle, not for Mom, and certainly not for me. For Jackie. I want Rosy to keep talking forever. She's making Jackie feel this way *for me*. Jackie cares about me, Jake Withers, enough to cry.

"Lord, your daddy used to be in here almost every night, Jake. Jack and Cokes. He's a Jack and Coke man. Never seen him drink anything else. He never plays pool like a lot of the other guys. Shoots some darts, though, once in a while. Used to be pretty good, but seems he lost interest. Truth be told, seems he lost interest in this place altogether. Kind of a shame. I liked havin' your daddy around, to tell you the truth. He wasn't always the greatest tipper, but he's a helluva nice guy and good company to have in this place on a slow night." Rosy puts her hands around her mouth like a megaphone and yells toward the bar, "I'll be right there, Gary! Keep your pants on, ya old drunk!" A squat, bald man in a tight shirt waves from the bar and takes a seat in the stool I was sitting in earlier. Rosy slides to the outside of the booth and puts both palms on the table. "I gotta get back to the grind, Jake, but I just want you to know I'm thinkin' about you. I could lose my job for servin' you, 'specially with how drunk you got, but how could I say no, considerin' your situation. Hell, a little booze'll probably do ya some good, get ya thinkin' about somethin' else for a while. Now, I never knew your mother, Jake, and I s'pose I don't know you too well, either, but Calvin Withers is a fine man, no matter what anyone says, and any son of his is just fine by me. If there's ever anything I can do for you or your family, Jake, you know where to find me. And I mean that from the bottom of my heart. I absolutely mean it." She pats me on the shoulder and tousles my hair a little, then stands up and offers Jackie a hand. Jackie shakes it. "And it's very nice to meet you, Jake's girlfriend. You sure are a pretty little thing. Treat him right, will ya? He's had a rough time of it, but I s'pose you know that." Rosy waddles away from the booth and I turn my attention back to Jackie. She didn't bother correcting Rosy about not being my girlfriend. That's got to be a good thing, right?

Jackie's still crying—definitely not sobbing or anything, but crying just the same. Her cheeks are pink and her mouth hangs open a little. She shakes her head slowly, once left, once right, then back to center. "I . . ." she begins, and her voice can't get past her throat. "I don't . . ." Without thinking, I reach my hands across the table and place them on top of hers. It seems like the right thing to do. She recoils, pulls her hands back. Grabs her purse and stands up abruptly. "Jake, I . . . I don't . . ." Thick, shiny tears form on the edges of her eyes and roll down her cheeks. "I'm really sorry, Jake. I didn't know." She shakes her head again, left, right, left, center, then turns and runs from the bar.

Chapter 12

Rosy lets me hang out and sober up a little while she counts the till and sweeps the floor. Not that it does much good. She insists on giving me a ride home, but I convince her that I'm okay, that the walking will do me some good, sober me up before I get home to Mom. I'm still plenty drunk when I walk out the door, but at least I can walk. Sort of.

The night has cooled off even more, so even though I don't accept Rosy's ride home, I'm happy to accept the jacket she offers me, even if it is purple and way too small.

Main Street is morgue silent; the town of Browerton is already asleep. I can't stop thinking about what Jackie said before she ran out of the bar. What did she mean? She said she didn't know, but she did. I know I was pretty drunk, but I'm positive I told her about Kyle the other night at the rock. Did she forget? Was she ignoring me? What the hell happened?

I stumble down the sidewalk, catching an occasional glimpse of my reflection in a storefront window. I see a lanky bum; a homeless, downtrodden misfit in a purple women's coat. The image strikes me funny and I laugh out loud, harder and longer than I've laughed in days. I laugh until my eyes fill with tears. Until, unable to walk further, I fall to my knees, and my laughter turns to sobs. I don't sob for Kyle, I don't sob for Mom, I don't sob for Dad. I hate myself because I sob for me. I sob for my fucking self. What is wrong with me? Just what the fuck is wrong with me? I can't even cry for my dead brother, can't even feel that he's dead. I cry because of his death, sure, but not because he didn't get to live the life he deserved. Because his death has inconvenienced *me*. His death has fucked *my* life up and made *me* feel out of control, not like I ever felt like I had control in the first place. *I deserve to have a dead brother. He didn't deserve to die, but it had to happen. I needed to be punished because I'm a selfish asshole. I deserve to have a crazy mother. I deserve to have a fucked-up father who barely knows he has a family. I brought this on them all. God doesn't kill the little brothers of good people. He kills the little brothers of selfish, unfeeling*

75

pricks like me. People who deserve it. I killed Kyle. I might as well have wrapped my hands around his little neck and squeezed, might as well have reached into his throat and pulled the air from his lungs, because it's my fault. My. Fault.

I've never been in a fight in my life, but the rage and hatred boils inside of me until it's the only thing I want, the only thing I need. I've always been too afraid of fighting—too afraid of everything, really—but now I don't fear it. I'd gladly wing a haymaker at the biggest, meanest guy I could find, and relish every blow he dealt.

Before I know what I'm doing enough to stop myself, it's already too late. My fist slams into my face again and again, knuckles against cheek, against jaw, against eye sockets. *Fuck you. You did this.* Over and over, my fist finds its mark. I don't feel blood on my face, but I see it streaming down, hitting the sidewalk and splattering in tiny drops. Forming rivulets in the cracks and fissures of the cold concrete. I don't remember making the choice, but now that I've begun to smash, to maul myself, I know why I must continue, and I can't stop.

Each blow makes me angrier, more pitiful, less forgivable. After several minutes, I slump to the ground, exhausted, lying on my side. My reflection in the storefront window shows my shoulder moving up and down with each breath, so I know I'm not dead. I've stopped not because I've had all I deserve, but because my body has given out.

With my last ounces of energy, I drag myself closer to the store window, fingertips digging into dry, cold concrete. The sickly yellow light of a streetlamp directly overhead reveals that my reflection is what it should be: a monster, barely human. My right eye is closed and my cheekbones, once sharp and prominent, have nearly disappeared beneath tight, swollen flesh. A wide ribbon of dried blood cakes the skin from the right side of my bottom lip to the tip of my chin. My left eyebrow is split open, gaping like a squinting, inhuman eye. In some sick way, I'm impressed with the damage I've done to myself. Amazed that I could affect anything in this world so fully, even if only myself, my face. I've become someone else.

Dragging myself into the nearest shadow, I roll into a ball, hunched up in the Radio Shack doorway. At least I'll be somewhat hidden from view in case a cop drives by. If I can just get some sleep here for a few hours, I can get up and walk home in the morning.

I'm not sure if I've been sleeping or not when a car pulls up to the curb right in front of me. The headlights click off but the engine keeps running. The driver's side door opens and closes, but my vision is still too blurry to make out the figure that exits the car and runs—*click clack click*—around the car and to the sidewalk. Not until she is kneeling next to me, picking my head up off my chest, do I see that it's Jackie.

"Oh my God, Jake!" she yells, stumbling backward. "What happened? Who the hell did this to you?"

"Me."

"Tell me what happened, Jake. *Right. Fucking. Now!*" she screams. "Who did this?"

"Me," I say. "I did. Already tol' you."

"*You? You* did?" she asks, pacing, hands on hips. "*You* did this to your*self?* Why? What the hell is *wrong* with you?"

I open my mouth to answer, to say something, but I can't. I just exhale and shake my head. What the hell do I say? How do I explain this? I'm not even sure I want her to know why I did it, even if she would understand.

"The fuck?" I mumble. "Howya find me?"

"Well . . . I wasn't going to *leave* you, Jake," she says. "You were way too drunk to walk home. Definitely way too drunk to get away with it if a cop saw you, and probably too drunk to physically even get yourself there. I've been driving around for like a half-hour looking for you. And now this? *This?* What the hell am I supposed to do? What?" She starts to cry into her hands, still pacing back and forth on the sidewalk, her high-heeled shoes *click-clack*ing on the pavement.

It all feels like too much. I can't say anything to make her stop. And why should I? Why is everything always *my* fault, like *I'm* the one who needs to fix everyone's fucking problems? I want her to stop crying, but what the fuck am *I* supposed to do about it? And why's she feeling so damn sorry for herself, like she's got it so fucking rough? *I'm* the one she should be feeling bad for. I'm the one with the dead brother and the crazy mom and the drunk dad. I'm the one whose dad doesn't own a fucking bank and who doesn't get a fucking car or five thousand fucking dollars or whatever just because it's my goddamn birthday. And we are, both of us, sobbing like fucking babies and I just want to go home. Go home and sleep for the next week, month, year, sleep for the rest of my fucking life because it's just too damn much. All of it. Just. Too. Damn. Much.

Jackie crouches down in front of me and puts her hands under my armpits. "Come on, drunky," she says. "Let's get you out of here before we both get arrested." I do what I can to help her pick me up, try to hold as much of my own weight as I can, but I'm pretty sure she's taking the brunt of it. Good thing I weigh 150 pounds soaking wet. Hell, I probably weigh less than she does, not that I'd ever tell her that. She pretty much drags me to the passenger's side of her car, opens the door, and pours me in. I hit my head on the car as I drop into the seat, but I can barely feel anything; my face is numb.

Even with my closed eye and blurred vision I can see that Jackie takes off the wrong way down Main Street—away from my house.

"Where we goin'?" I ask.

"You're going to come stay with me tonight," she says.

"Your house?" I ask. "We're going all the way to Clouton?" It's all of 12 miles, but right now that feels too far.

"Yeah," she says. "Don't worry about it. Just close your eyes and get some sleep or something."

"Why we goin' to Clouton? My house jus' up the road." Every sentence is involuntarily punctuated with a loud hiccup.

"I just think," she starts. Then, "I don't want to talk about it now, but there's something I need to tell you."

"Jus' tell me," I slur. "Tell me right *now*."

"No," she says firmly. "Not now. Not tonight. You need to sleep and sober up and be . . . I don't know . . . fucking *present*. You need to be *all there* for this. Trust me."

"Is it about *him*?"

"*Who?*"

"That ape-man," I say. "Your boyfriend or whatever."

"What the fuck are you talking about, Jake?" She's getting genuinely pissed but I'm too drunk to recoil like I normally would.

"That big, toady bastard," I say. "Jennifer or Sally or whatever the fuck his name is."

"Ashlee?"

"Sure," I say. "Ashlee."

"What about Ashlee?" she asks. "He's not my boyfriend. Not that it'd be any of your fucking business if he was."

"You guys're pretty close," I say, and I'm pressing now, egging her on. "Pretty damn friendly."

"What the *fuck* is that supposed to mean?" she asks. "What the hell is *wrong* with you, Jake? Is this how you always think but you only let it out when you're drunk? God."

"Yeah, maybe," I say, slumping low in my seat. "Probably is. Whatever. I jus' like you. Wish you were my girlfriend and don' know why you wanna hang out with some toady meathead," I say, and I'm too drunk to care if I sound like an idiot. "Tha's all." At this point, her ideal response would be *I really like you too, Jake. In fact, I love you. Of course I want to be your girlfriend. Take me in your arms and make love to me, you scrawny, beautiful little monkey boy.*

Instead, she drives on in silence. Clears her throat. Doesn't look at me.

Chapter 13

I wake up slowly. My throat is so dry it hurts and my lips feel glued shut with thick, tacky saliva. Peeling my face from the vinyl of Jackie's car seat, it hits me all at once where I am. I can't quite remember what happened last night or how I got here, but I know I'm in Jackie's car. My face feels hot and tight, and I reach up and graze two fingertips around my left eye. I suck in through my teeth and pull my hand away. I flip down the car's visor but there's no mirror. My whole face hurts. I sit upright in the seat and, once my eyes adjust to the bright sunlight, I realize that I don't recognize my surroundings. Out the window to my right, I see grass and a small treeline, maybe 50 yards away. I can't quite make out the reflection of my face in the window. The view out the windshield shows a small, one-level house painted a sickly blue/green that I've only seen on a color crayon. To my left is—Jackie. The driver's seat is reclined so far back that it's nearly flat and she's curled up almost into a ball with her back to me. I'm not sure if I should wake her up or not, but hopefully she can tell me what's going on and how I can get a drink of water before I *die*. My throat feels like a tumbleweed.

I reach over and poke the small of Jackie's back with one finger. Nothing. I do it again, harder. She slaps at my hand half-heartedly and mutters a few syllables but doesn't stir. I poke again and her head lifts suddenly from the seat. She sits up quickly and turns to me, eyes half-closed.

"Oh, hey," she says. Her eyes open wide and her motherly instincts kick in. "Ohhhhhh . . ." she whimpers. "You are a *mess*. You look absolutely horrible. Oh, my god. Does it *hurt*?"

"Yes," I say. "And thanks. 'You look horrible' is one of my favorite things to hear when I wake up."

"Sorry," she says. "How'd you sleep?"

"Judging from the cramp in my neck, I'd say I slept like a Picasso painting." I contort my body and jut my neck painfully to the side as a

79

visual. Jackie laughs a little but I'm not sure she gets the Picasso joke. "I need something to drink." It comes out as a croak. "Bad."

"Okay," she says. "Let me run inside and get you something."

"Where are we anyway?" I ask. "Whose house is this?" But she's already out of her seat and closing the door and I'm not sure if she heard me. It's hot and stuffy in the car and it looks like there's a nice breeze outside. I open my door and, with effort, lift myself from the seat. The cool breeze hits me and I feel better almost immediately. A little better. Still thirsty as hell and it seems I have a headache I didn't notice until I stood up, but the breeze feels good against my bruised face.

On the other side of the treeline I can make out the shape of another small house. An older man in bib overalls kneels in a small garden, digging with a hand shovel. He stops for a moment and looks at me but doesn't wave. It's like he sees me but doesn't want to. A narrow, dusty alley runs through the lot behind the houses, and both backyards are littered with debris: engine parts, a rusty wheelbarrow, an old brick-colored picnic table with peeling paint. I'm standing in the world's only trailer park with stationary homes.

Jackie comes out of the house and hands me a green plastic cup. Water. I take it from her and gulp most of it down. I pause and offer it to her, but she shakes her head. I finish it and wish I had more.

"Thanks," I say. "For the water and for taking care of me last night. I don't remember much, but you obviously didn't let me die. I'll know what to say if my mom asks me what I'm thankful for during the Thanksgiving prayer." Jackie forces a smile. I suddenly remember last night—Sammy's, Ashlee, Rosy, no sign of Dad. I want to push it from my mind because it hurts just to exist right now, but *what am I going to do about Mom? The funeral is tomorrow.*

"Where the hell are we?" I ask.

"You should come inside," she says and takes my hand. "Let's get you cleaned up a little."

Inside the house, Jackie pulls me down the stairs and into a small bathroom. Positioning herself between me and the mirror, she doesn't let me pass.

"Are you ready to see yourself?" she asks.

"Yeah," I say. "Actually, I'm pretty excited about it."

"Are you sure? It's pretty bad."

"Yeah. Sure, I'm sure." She lets go of my arm.

I look in the mirror and see the elephant man. I expected it to be bad, but if I died right now, they'd have to bust out the dental records to identify me. Nearly the entire left side of my face is dark purple and shiny. The area around my eye is more swollen than I had even believed

Just Jake | 81

human flesh could be—something between a golf ball and a tennis ball is growing beneath the skin just beside my eye, trying to break through like a face-hugger from *Aliens*.

Jackie pulls a jar of cotton balls from under the sink, dips one in alcohol and touches it to the large cut above my eye. I wince a little, but it's not too bad. It feels good to know that whatever was growing in there will be dead. Even though I have a million questions, I mostly keep my mouth shut and let Jackie clean me up. When she's done with the alcohol, she wets a cloth under the sink and wipes my face gently. It's not quite the full body sponge bath I could go for but it feels good.

"What's going on, Jackie?" I ask. "Can you please tell me? I really feel like something weird is going on." She's silent for a moment, chewing her lower lip. She looks like she wants to be somewhere else. "Is this *your* house? Is it?"

She tells me she's not sure what to say, not sure if she should say anything at all. Then she takes me by the hand again and leads me, slowly, out of the dark basement and up into the light.

Upstairs, we navigate through the kitchen on a narrow path, littered on each side with dirty laundry, empty beer cans, crumpled fast food wrappers. The counter is piled with weeks' worth of dirty dishes. A cloud of tiny insects rises from the sink as we pass. The refrigerator hums loudly and a sour, rotting smell hangs in the air.

In the living room, a woman is asleep on a drab sofa. Near her head, a wild puff of cotton batting protrudes from a tear in the sofa's arm. A large brownish stain almost covers the throw pillow near her feet. Oprah grins from the fuzzy, black and white TV screen. The woman turns her head slightly and I see her face; it's the beehive hairdo lady that we saw in the Quikmart parking lot. Jackie's mom's friend from the hospital. I want to ask her where we are, whose house this is, but then I know, without a doubt, that this *is* Jackie's home. The woman on the couch is her mother. Jackie's face is a mix of embarrassment and comfort. She doesn't want me to see her home like this, but this is how it is. Her father does not own a bank. Her mother is not a nurse. Her family does not spend weekends at a lush cabin on a remote, clear-watered lake. It's all been a lie. All of it. *Why did she bring me here? Why would she try so hard to convince me that she was someone else, then just bring me here out of the blue and shatter the fantasy?*

Jackie enters the living room and kneels down next to her mother while I stand in the doorway, uncomfortable and wishing, for what feels like the first time in years, that I was at home. Jackie whispers into her mother's ear and she opens her eyes, blinks twice, hard, and looks around the room. Her eyes fall on me for a long moment before she looks away. Jackie whispers again and her mother whispers back. Jackie kisses her mother's cheek. Pats her head and tells her to go back to sleep. Jackie stands up, walks across the room, and sits in a small wooden chair. She motions to a light blue recliner and tells me to sit. Again, something tells me I don't want to be here. My feet want to run for the door and out into the day, down the block, out of town, back home to Browerton. But I cross the room. Sit. I can't sit still, though; can't get comfortable. I'm fidgeting like a kid in the principal's office.

From down a hallway outside the living room, I hear the sound of a toilet flushing, then a running faucet. The door opens and a man steps into the hallway.

He's noticeably slimmer than the last time I saw him and he's wearing a long sleeve button-up shirt. His face is clean-shaven. He's almost in the living room, no more than ten feet in front of me, when our eyes meet. I feel like I'm floating above the ceiling, watching my life happen, and I wonder if he feels the same. He speaks first, breaks the silence.

"Jake."

"Hi, Dad."

Chapter 14

I feel like I'm spinning and I might be sick. Like a giant hand has come out of the sky, grabbed me by the collar, and dropped me in the middle of the Twilight Zone. I'm in Jackie's run-down, warzone of a house and my dad is standing not ten feet in front of me. I have nothing to say. I'm waiting for myself to snap awake, maybe wake up back home in my bed or in Jackie's car or even on the sidewalk in front of the Radio Shack, fucking *anywhere*, as long as I wake up, and right now. Dad pulls a pack of cigarettes from his shirt pocket and lights one. Takes a drag, then leans against the doorway and crosses his arms. *How can he be so fucking relaxed right now? After what he did to us? To me, Kyle, and Mom? His youngest son is dead, died in Mom's arms, and he doesn't even know it.*

"Kyle's dead!" I blurt out before running from the room, shouldering my dad aside. I'm out the door and sitting on the trunk of Jackie's car with my face buried in my hands before I even realize what I've done. Behind me, the front door opens and closes and I know it's him. He walks up behind me tentatively. I imagine him leaning against the back door of Jackie's car, arms crossed, just like he did inside. That same relaxed, cocky stance. But I don't turn around to see if I'm right. I feel numb and sick and not real. *What the fuck is my dad doing at Jackie's house?* I ask myself, but I know. *Fucking Jackie's mom, that's what. Mom was right—Dad does have himself a girlfriend in Clouton. Tthat's why he hasn't been at Sammy's. Hasn't been at home either.*

"So you finally got yourself a girlfriend, huh?" he says finally. "Jackie's a cutie, too."

"Fuck you," I say and no part of me regrets it. *How could he say something like that right now? Just start in with the playful father/son bullshit when his son is dead and none of us really know what the fuck is going on?*

"Okay," he says. "Alright. I suppose I deserve that."

"Goddamn right you do." He comes around the back of the car and leans on the trunk a foot or so to my right. I look straight ahead.

"You look like hell warmed over," he says. "What happened to your face? You all of sudden turn into the fightin' type?"

"Did you even hear what I said in there? Kyle's dead. He died at the hospital a few days ago. Mom brought him in for pneumonia again and . . ."

"I know, Jake." My head feels like it's swelling up like a balloon and my heart is trying to push thick, black tar though my veins.

"You *know?*" I ask, and I turn to him, curse him out with my eyes. "You know Kyle is dead? You know about this and you didn't come home? What the . . . how the fuck? What the hell is wrong with you?"

"I saw it in the paper, Jake," he says. "I . . ."

"You *what?* You fucking *what?* You fucking knew that your son was dead, your fucking baby, and you couldn't even face us then? Couldn't even come see your family? See how we're doing? It's too fucking much to ask of you to just . . . just . . . . I don't know, *be* a fucking father for a little while? Remember that you actually *have* a family?"

"You wouldn't have wanted me there," he says. He averts his eyes, inspects his brown, scuffed boots. He sounds defeated. *Honest.*

"I don't know if what we want matters right now," I say. "I know that we *need* you right now. I know that your fucking family needs you. What else do we have, Dad? After Grandma and Grandpa died and . . . you know Mom doesn't have anyone anymore at the hospital . . . . and you're never around. Mom isn't okay, Dad. She's not okay at all. She's sick again and I don't know what to do. How am I supposed to do this, Dad? I'm sixteen fucking years old. I'm a *kid,* Dad. I'm still a fucking kid and I shouldn't have to . . ." and then I'm crying. Bawling. Part of me wants him to hold me, to put his arm around me and pull me to his chest like a father should do for his son at a moment like this, but part of me wants to keep him distant. To see what he has done to his family and know that it's his fault and that it's too late to change it because the damage has been done.

He doesn't put his arm around me or hug me or touch me at all. Just stands still with his hands in his pockets, looking at his work boots.

"Nah, you don't need me, Jake," he says. "You haven't needed me for a while." I want to agree with him—tell him that he's right, that I need a drunken bastard like him in my life like I need a cancerous tumor. And I suppose he is right, in a way. I didn't need a father, really. I'm still here. I'm fucked up and I am what I am and I've pretty much got no family left, but I'm here.

"It sure as hell wasn't easy without you around," I say, still sniffling. "When you're gone and mom's sick and Kyle's . . . well, Kyle's Kyle . . .

and now he's gone and . . . I was alone, Dad. I was always fucking alone, whether you knew it or not. And it *is* your fault. *It is.* Because you could have been there. I needed you—we needed you—more than you know. And we need you now. I need you to come home, Dad. Tonight. Right now. Mom is bad. She doesn't even know Kyle's gone. She talks like he's right there and she tells me to look after him when she goes to work and she pours him bowls of cereal for God's sake. Sets a bowl full of cereal on his tray and waits for it to fucking disappear. She needs you, Dad. Some part of you has to know that. Some part of you has to know that you are the only one who can make her better."

He shakes his head and sighs, deep and long and lonely.

"That's not true, Jake," he says. "There's a time it was true, but not anymore. Your mom and I . . . Look, it was you and Kyle kept her going, for a long time now. She doesn't need me, Jake. Not for a long time. Who she needs is you."

"Fuck that!" I yell. "She doesn't need me. Hasn't needed me ever! She barely fucking knows I'm there most of the time. It's always Kyle this and Kyle that and *goo-goo-goo* and shit! I go to work and I go to school and I take care of Kyle and she doesn't even look at me most of the time." I stop to see if he has anything to say, but he just pulls a cigarette from his pocket and lights it. "Kyle's funeral is tomorrow, Dad. You need to be there. You need to come home tonight, Dad, and talk to Mom and get her there and tell her you love her and make her okay. She'll listen to you, Dad. She loves you. Doesn't she? I mean, doesn't she love you?"

He shakes his head, lets out another of those longs sighs. "I don't know, Jake. I don't know much about your mother anymore. The woman I married has been as good as gone for years already. I suppose she's in there somewhere yet, but I ain't seen her in an awfully long time."

"Just come home, Dad, okay? If not tonight, at least come to the funeral and talk to Mom there. Or after. Something. Just come home." Part of me hates myself for pleading with him like this. I would like to have kept the ball in my court, kept screaming at him until he had to do what I say.

"I just don't know, Jake," he says, "if I'm part of that family anymore." He looks at me quickly, then looks away again. Kicks a pebble with his boot. "I'm not sure there's a place for me anymore. I'm not sure I want a place anymore." I want to scream at him again, scream some sense into him, but suddenly I am drained of energy. I could lie down on the hot pavement at my feet and fall asleep for days. Lie down and die.

Dad turns and walks back to the house. His last words ring in my ears.

I'm not sure I want a place anymore.

Chapter 15

The leaves on the trees that line Highway 17 from Clouton to Browerton have already begun to change. Oranges, yellows, and browns mostly, but the occasional tree decked out in bright red leaves sticks out like a sore thumb. The ditches are littered with brown, decaying leaves, plastic bags, the occasional discarded shoe. The mile marker signs are closer together than usual and they come at me in segmented time—*click, click, click*—like a badly edited horror movie. A flock of Canada geese rises from the reservoir a few miles out of town as we pass. They fall into a 'V', lazy at first, then tighter and head south until I lose them somewhere above. On the other side of the reservoir, a deer, little more than a fuzzy brown speck, drinks, raising its head every few seconds to survey its surroundings, check for predators.

Jackie and I don't speak the whole ride home. In fact, I'm pretty sure we didn't speak before getting in the car either. A few minutes after my Dad went inside, Jackie came out and got in the car. I got in after her and she started the car without speaking and left for Browerton.

I'm still too tired to think. Too tired to put the pieces of this puzzle together—Jackie, me, my dad, Mom, Kyle. It's all a puzzle and it's too much for me right now. All of this is too much. I need to sleep.

Jackie asks if I want a ride to my car and I tell her to just bring me home. When she pulls into the driveway, I'm relieved to see Mom's car. Jackie remembers to hand me my keys before weakly muttering that she's sorry. I get out of the car and don't say anything. Close the door and walk toward the house. I don't know what to say to her right now. I'm too tired and confused to even know if I have anything to say.

In the living room, Mom is sitting on the couch watching TV. She smiles at me when I first walk into the room, and it's nice to see her looking happy, even if it is only for the split second before she really sees my face.

"What the hell happened to you?" she says, and she sounds more angry than concerned. Somehow accusatory.

"Hey, Ma," I say. "It's nice to see you, too." She's still wearing that pink robe and I wonder again if she actually showed up at work that way.

"Did you get in a fight?" she asks. "Who was it? Must've been more than one of 'em by the looks of you."

"No, Ma. I didn't get in a fight. Listen, what happened to me doesn't matter. We need to talk. About something else."

"You look tired, Jake. Maybe you should get some sleep."

"I *am* tired," I say. "This has been really hard for me, Mom. Harder than you know, I think." I'm at my wit's end. I don't know what else to do but just talk to her. Tell her the truth about Kyle—make her understand it. Tell her and tell her and tell her until she has to face it.

"Uh oh, Jake," she says. "Problems with your pretty little girlfriend? I hope not."

"No, Ma," I say. "It's not that." I take a deep breath and it's one of those *here goes nothing* moments. I'm not sure how to begin. "Ma, where's Kyle? How come he's not here today?" She looks at his chair, sitting just a few feet in front of the couch, still facing the TV. "Hmmm," she starts. "You know, Jake, I'm not sure, but I guess Helen must have taken him to school."

"No, Ma," I say. "He's not at school. It's Sunday. And school doesn't start for a couple weeks yet." She looks around the room, genuinely confused.

"Well, I don't know, Jake," she says. "You had him last. You fed him his breakfast while I was at work yesterday, didn't you? What did you do with him? He must be in bed. Is he taking his nap?"

"No, Mom," I say. "He's not taking his nap." She's doesn't normally like to be touched when she's sick because she doesn't trust people, but I take my chances sliding toward her on the couch and sort of putting my arm around her back. "He's gone, Mom. Remember? Don't you remember? At the hospital? Kyle died, Mom. He's not coming back."

"No," she says, shaking her head slowly at first, then faster. "No. Nono."

"And you're sick again Mom," I say. "You need help. I don't know if you stopped taking your medicine or what, but you're sick again and I don't know what to do. What am I supposed to do, Ma?"

"What I want to know is what you *did*!" she screams. "What did you do with Kyle? Did you hurt him, Jake? Where is he?"

"He's gone, Mom," I say. "And I didn't do it. No one did it. It's no one's fault, Mom." I hate feeling like I'm the parent—like I have to take care of her. But I've felt like that a lot in my life. "What about Helen,

Mom? Have you talked to Helen since Kyle . . . I mean, have you talked to Helen lately?"

"Oh, not for awhile I guess," she says, and she's already forgotten about blaming me for Kyle's absence. "Not for a few days, anyway."

"What about anyone else, Ma?" I ask. "Has anyone else been by lately? Have you talked to anyone? What about at work?" I'm trying to figure out where I can go for help. I've never had to be the one to help Mom when she's sick before. She hasn't been this bad ever that I know of, and she hasn't been bad at all for years, and Dad has pretty much taken care of it before.

"They sent me home," she says and she laughs a little. "I showed up, on time and everything, and they asked me to go home. Told me I didn't have to come back until I heard from them again. That I could take as much time as I needed." She shakes her head and giggles again. She sounds like a little girl.

"Has anyone stopped by the house with gifts or anything? Came by and said they were sorry?"

"Sorry for what, silly?" she asks. "But since you mention it, yeah. A couple of the neighbors came by. I think Al from next door stopped by maybe yesterday and some of the other neighbors from down the street—Mr. and Mrs. Braun and Jessi Burbank, your old babysitter. They stopped by, oh I don't know, day before yesterday. Jessi brought a pie I think. I'm sure it's still in the fridge if you want some. Let me get you some." She stands up and leaves the room.

"Ma, no," I say. "Ma, it's fine—I don't want any pie. I'd rather just talk to you." But it's too late. She's gone. I'm lucky I was able to get her to listen for as long as I did. When she's sick, she's even more in her own world than usual and her mind goes where it wants to go. You can't stop it. No one can.

I want to just handle this on my own, somehow snap her out of this and make her see the truth without having to get the whole town involved. Maybe I should just get over it, but I guess I still live in some sort of fantasy world where everyone in town doesn't already know that my family is a mess. It'll be bad enough going back to school in two weeks and having to deal with everyone knowing that my brother just died. I don't want them whispering about my loony bin mom too. But I'm out of ideas. She won't listen to me. Dad won't come home and I can't do this alone. I pick up the phone.

"Hello?" She sounds as chipper as ever.

"Hey, Helen," I say. "It's Jake again."

"Oh." Her voice drops a little. "How are you, Jake?"

"Okay," I say. "Listen, Helen . . ."

Just Jake | 89

"And how about your mother, Jake? How is she? Is she home?"

"Yeah," I say. "Yeah, she is."

"Could I talk to her a moment, Jake?" she asks. "Would you mind?"

"No," I say. "Actually, that's kind of why I called. But do you think you could, like, come over? I mean, instead of talk to her on the phone? Do you think you could come over and see her?"

"Well, of course, Jake," she says. "When shall I come?" *Shall.* Sometimes Helen cracks me up.

"Actually, soon would be great," I tell her. "Real soon. Like, now."

"Is there an emergency, Jake?" she asks. "Is everything okay?"

"Yeah. I mean, no. It's not . . ." and then I'm crying again. It doesn't come on in heaving sobs, but tears fill my eyes quickly and I need to get off the phone. "Just come quick, okay?"

"I'll be right there, Jake," she says, and I hang up.

In the kitchen, mom is digging through the cabinets, looking for a pie plate.

"Jake, what's wrong?" she asks. "Why are you crying?" I want to just hug her and tell her everything's going to be fine. I want to just leave the room and hide under my blankets until kingdom come. I want to just shoot myself.

"What's wrong with me, Mom?"

"What do you mean, Jake?" she says. "Nothing's wrong with you. You're fine." There's an edge of meanness in her voice—a kind of hiss that tells me I'm wrong to ask. "But why can't I help you, Mom? And even if I can't, why couldn't I find someone who could? Why did I let this . . .?"

"I have no idea what you're talking about," she says. "Stop crying. You stop crying right now, do you hear me? Stop it. STOP IT!" and she's screaming, slamming her fists against the refrigerator.

By the time the door bell rings and Helen comes up the stairs, Mom and I are collapsed on the kitchen floor, sobbing in each other's arms. It's the closest I remember being to my mother. And I don't mean just in the last few years, either; I mean *ever.* Helen runs to us, hands pressed to her cheeks. "Oh, no!" she says. "Oh, goodness!" and she squats down and wraps us both in her arms. Her perfume smells like church and her fake pearl necklace presses against my face. "Oh, goodness, you two!" she says. "Why didn't you call sooner, Jake? You two shouldn't be alone like this. You need support from your family and friends. I would have come right over, Jake, if you'd asked me." I know she's trying to help, but she only makes me feel worse. I could have called Helen. I could have told her to come over and help. Who did I think I was kidding? What could I possibly hide from her that she doesn't already know? She knows this family as well as anyone: how fucked up we are, how anything about us that seems normal is pretend—part of the front that we work so hard to put forward.

Helen squeezes us tighter and I'm closer still to my mother, the woman who has never really been my mother, the woman who only had enough love for one son, the woman who sometimes seems to see me, even love me, but only in moments when she's someone else.

Helen cries with us. We all three squeeze and rock back and forth and cry and things start to feel a little better in one way and a whole lot worse in another. I hear Helen mumble something about my beat up face, but she doesn't ask what happened. She doesn't seem surprised. I guess the outside of me finally matches the inside.

After what seems like a long time, we go into the living room and sit on the couch, with Mom in the middle and Helen and I on either end. We don't speak for quite a while and Mom eventually asks if anyone wants coffee and, ignoring the fact that we both say no, goes into the kitchen and starts a pot. Helen turns to me and speaks, hushed and hurried.

"How is she, Jake?" she asks. "I haven't spoken to her at length since . . . this whole thing."

"Bad," I say. "She needs help. I didn't . . . I didn't really know what to do."

"Well of course you didn't, you poor thing," she says, placing a hand on my shoulder. "Why, you're just a child, Jake. I know you've had to grow up faster than some, but this is too much for just one boy to handle alone." She looks over toward the kitchen, then back to me. "Is she sick again, Jake? Does she need to go in?"

"Yeah," I say. "Yeah, I think so. She doesn't know."

"She never knows, Jake. She can't tell when she's sick. That's why she's so lucky to have such a wonderful son to help her know when she needs help."

"No," I say. "No, I don't mean that. She doesn't know about Kyle. She doesn't even know he's gone."

"She doesn't . . ." Helen starts, but stumbles on her words. "She thinks . . ."

"Yeah," I say. "She thinks he's still here. Still buys him cereal and pushes his chair in front of the T.V. Turns on his favorite shows for him. Talks to him. Tells me to feed him or put him to bed or whatever. She doesn't know."

Helen just nods her head a little. Lets out a deep sigh and opens her mouth a little, but doesn't speak.

"What?" I ask. "What were you going to say?"

"Well," she says, "I don't know, Jake. This is hard. This won't be easy at all. I don't know if you've ever been around when she's been taken in, but she can be a real bearcat about the whole thing. Remember, now, she doesn't know anything's wrong. She doesn't think she needs help. When she gets bad like this, she thinks we're the ones who need help and she's the only one who knows what's going on. Imagine feeling like everyone's out to get you and you're the only one in the world who understands the truth. That's how it is for your mom when she gets sick, Jake. Or that's how I imagine it, anyway."

Although I don't tell Helen, I can't help but think that I know that feeling too. Maybe not as well as my mom does, and maybe not even in the same way, but I know what it feels like to feel like you're in the world alone and no one gets you but yourself.

"And of course, this time, Jake, there's the problem of the funeral," she says. "Do we bring her to the funeral? Make her face the truth that way? Or would it be too much? And if we don't bring her, will she be upset that she missed it once she comes back around?"

"I don't know," I say, and I don't. I really don't know.

"Who's her doctor, Jake?" she asks. "Does she have a doctor we can call? Someone who's dealt with her illness before and knows what to do in these situations?"

Again, I tell Helen that I don't know. Maybe Helen doesn't know how invisible I was in this family. I'm not sure how she could have missed it, but she doesn't seem to realize that I was left out of these things. I know almost nothing about my mother's illness or my father's past or what my brother wanted out of life or anything. I don't even know who I am, what I want.

"Well, I'm just going to pick one then," she says. "I'm going to call a doctor, Jake, and we'll get to the bottom of this." She stands up to leave the room but pauses. Turns around and faces me. "You've done nothing wrong, Jake. None of this is your fault. You did the right thing by calling me and there was nothing else you could have done. I don't want you blaming yourself for this or anything that's happened with your family. It's not your fault. None of it is and it never has been and I don't want you sitting there thinking it is. Do you understand that?"

I nod. She leaves the room.

She doesn't see how it's my fault. But how could she? It's nice to hear the things she said, but she's not the one I need to hear them from.

The next couple hours go by like a blur. The ambulance comes and two men and one woman come inside the house to get Mom. She screams and cries and acts like the little girl from The Exorcist. It's one of the most frightening things I've ever seen and I hope to never see it again. She screams at me to call the cops because they're hurting her, trying to kill her, trying to take her and lock her up and never let her out. Part of me feels like I should fight for her, like she's my mother and I have to listen to her even when I know that what's happening is the best thing for us all. Eventually, the two men hold Mom down while the woman gives her a shot in her shoulder. A tranquilizer of some kind. She thrashes and screams and spits the whole time, but after awhile, she calms down and her eyes glaze over. I watch her change from demon to zombie right before my eyes.

Helen asks me if I want to go along in the ambulance and I shake my head no. The three paramedics or whatever they are take Mom outside and I watch out the picture window as they herd her into the back of the ambulance. Helen climbs in after them. The ambulance pulls out into the street, and I am alone.

Chapter 16

The doorbell rings a little after 8:00 a.m. and I almost don't answer it. When I open the door, Helen is standing on the stoop in a black dress and a little black hat with a flat top. For once, she is somber; for once, she doesn't try to act like everything's okay.

"Well, good morning, Jake," she says. "I didn't expect to find you up yet."

"Couldn't sleep," I tell her, turning to walk up the stairs. She follows.

"Aren't you tired, Jake?" she asks. "You sure look tired." *Of course I'm tired*, I think. *I've never been so exhausted in my life. But in case you haven't noticed, my entire world has pretty much fallen apart and I don't even know if I want to be a part of it anymore.* She'd freak if I told her that I spent the entire night sitting up on the couch staring at the wall, thinking and not thinking at the same time. Trying to decide just what it is I do in this world and whether it's important. Whether it makes any difference to anyone.

"Well, I just thought I'd come over to make sure you were up and ready," she says, starting a pot of coffee. "I know today's going to be a hard day, Jake. It's going to be hard for all of us, but I thought I'd see if I couldn't make it a little easier for you." She waits a moment for me to speak, but I don't.

"I thought maybe we could see if we can't fix up your face a little," she says. "An old woman like me might not be good for much, but one thing I can do is put on make-up." She lowers a small, black leather bag onto the table. "I've got some stuff here that'll have you looking good as new."

Normally I would protest the idea of having make-up applied to my face, but this morning I don't have the energy. If it will make Helen feel better to know that I won't be scaring everyone away from the funeral with my swollen, discolored face, then I guess she can have her fun. I really don't care. She asks me if I'd planned to take a shower this

93

morning before the funeral, but I don't answer. She wets a washcloth at the kitchen sink and wipes my face gently, then dries it with a towel. She bites her lower lip and squints as she applies all different kinds of make-up to my cheeks, my eyes, my forehead. A couple of times she stops and her brow furrows and she says "hmmmm" before dipping another brush in another color and dabbing at my face with it.

"There," she proclaims after a few minutes. "Not too bad, if I do say so myself. A little swollen still, but the bruising is as good as gone." She takes out a little round mirror and holds it in front of my face. I look like a mannequin—like something inanimate, unreal. A plastic doll. A puppet, incapable of moving or speaking without a hand to guide me.

The next several hours move in frames, alternately too fast and too slow, but either way not quite real. Helen makes me breakfast and I pick at it. Helen asks me questions and I don't answer them. Helen tells me things will get better and I don't believe her. At some point during the morning I go to my room and get dressed—a black button-down shirt and khaki pants. Helen wets my hair and fiddles with it until she seems satisfied. She sees my Chuck Taylors and asks if I have nicer shoes. Dress-up shoes. I don't answer and she drops it.

We arrive at the funeral in Helen's car, a newish Oldsmobile, immaculate inside and out. We're over an hour early. The parking lot is empty. Inside the church, I sit in a pew in the last row. Helen goes off to the basement, mumbling something about lunch after the service. No one else is here. The church room is big, bigger even than I remember from my childhood. We were never a churchgoing family exactly, but we came on holidays—Christmas and Easter like the other heathens. The ceiling and walls are painted a bright, robin's egg blue. Huge beams flank the arched walls, meeting at the top in a single beam, wide as a tabletop, that runs the entire length of the room. On each wall, huge stained-glass windows depict scenes from the Bible: Moses holding the commandments over his head. The snake, bright green with a red tongue and human eyes, wrapped around a tree trunk. Two disciples whispering, wide-eyed, as Jesus walks across the water. I stand and walk to the front of the church. The room swallows me with its silence, its sheer size and openness. I climb a set of three stairs, carpeted blood red, that lead to the altar. Jesus himself, grey and cracked, at least eight feet tall, hangs, defeated, from the splintered cross. Small rivulets of painted blood mar his grey body, running down his side, his legs, his face. His eyes are half-open inches below a crown of braided and tangled thorns. He looks helpless. Dead. Too weak to help me or anyone. Mom always believed in God. Always said prayers with me when I was little, before Kyle was born. Does she still believe now? After everything that has happened, could she still believe that some all-powerful creator is looking down on us? That he actually cares about what happens to us?

I kneel down on the red carpet and place my forehead against the smooth wooden railing in front of me. I suppose most would see it as a sign of reverence, but it's nothing more than fatigue. Complete exhaustion. It hurts to care and I'm not even sure what I should care about. Right here, right now, in this holy place, this place of worship, kneeling before this massive statue of a god, a savior, I feel as hollow and numb and dead as I've ever felt. Kyle's coffin is somewhere in this building, I suppose, and I feel like I'm in it, too weak to even scratch at the wood to let the mourners know I'm alive.

Helen finds me in the front of the church, still kneeling, half asleep, and herds me into a pew. People start to show up and Helen greets them at the door, playing the part of mother of the deceased. The people look at me as they pass, on the way to their seats, but they don't speak. They try to let their faces do the talking, squeeze out grimaces and tears that are not quite real because they know how people are supposed to act at funerals. A few of the neighbors show up, a few teachers from school, one of my old babysitters. The church is too big. I don't care what Rosy says, there's no more than a handful of people in this town who give a damn about Kyle or my family. It feels like hours later when the service begins. Kyle's coffin—sealed, thank god—sits, massive and still, at the front of the church. Was it there all along?

The pastor drones in a low, somber voice and I hear him but don't listen. I'm trying to think about anything but Kyle laying there in that wooden box when a memory of him floods my mind, so real and intense that the space behind my eyes aches. I'm sitting at the piano, the bench pulled far to one side to make room for Kyle's chair next to me. I've lifted his left hand with my right, and brought it to the keyboard, where I form his hand into chords. I don't play a song really—a C, a D#, an E minor—but it's enough. He squirms in his chair like he always does when he's happy. His arm is heavy, his hand awkward and difficult to control, but I manage to gently move his fingers into the right spots and press them down—he's playing the notes and he knows it. Still squirming and bucking in his chair, he starts to moan, a low gurgle in his throat that grows higher, more urgent. He wants to play it. He wants to play The William Tell Overture. "It's too hard, Kyle," I tell him. "Too fast. I don't think we can do it. I can play it *for* you." He bucks harder, moans louder. I feel like he's communicating with me for the first time, like I really truly know what he wants. "Okay, buddy," I say. "We'll go for it. We'll give it a try." I slide the piano bench out of the way and move his chair over.

Standing behind him, I bring my arms around his body, picking up his left arm again and bringing it to the keyboard. It's a simplified version, stripped down to basic, two-note chords for the left hand while my right hand takes care of the fast stuff, but I'll be damned if we don't get it. Even if it's not quite right, no one can tell us that we're not playing his song. That *he's* not.

Notes ring out from the front of the church as the organist begins the next hymn and I know, suddenly and surely, as sure as I've ever known anything, what I must do. Helen touches my arm gently when I stand but I pay her no mind. I march out of the pew and down the long, wide aisle toward the front of the church. The pastor's voice cracks when he sees me, but he keeps singing. The organist, an older woman with greying hair, glances up at me as I approach. She stops playing and the voices die as she slides out of the bench, keeping her eyes on me as she shuffles away. I sit, and tongues of flame roll inside my chest, bolts of electricity spark and crackle down my arms and into my hands, and I play. I play as fast and as hard as I can, The William Tell Overture. Only the fast part, only the end. Kyle's coffin is ten feet away, outside my view, but no less real because of it, and I play. My hands are a blur on the keys, my fingers like machines, computerized pistons that operate separate from my mind, pumping up and down, back and forth over the keys. The electricity in my hands moves back up through my arms and into my chest where it burns again, a blazing hot flame that warms but does not destroy, and he's here with me, inside of me. Kyle's arms wrap around my body and he's guiding me, showing me the right notes, the right keys, showing me where the music is, and the world shuts off and there is only Kyle and me, and I cry. I cry for him, finally, for Kyle, my brother, trapped for all his life inside a shell, wanting only to be, to move, to speak, to play, to show. I throw my head back and sob, deep, guttural roars, and around me is only grey, and my hands, and Kyle's hands, and we play.

Back at home, I drift in and out of light sleep for most of the day, while Helen cleans up around the house, trying to make it look like civilized people live here. My sleep isn't deep enough to dream, and I think I'm thankful for that. One image keeps popping into my mind when I close my eyes: my father, partially hidden in shadow in the church's balcony. As I walked from the piano back to my pew, and the grey world slowly crept back into focus, I saw him. Leaned against a wall, in a back corner of the balcony, wearing the same button-down shirt I'd seen him in at Jackie's. I couldn't see his face really, but I know it was him. He was there. Too embarrassed or ashamed or whatever to really show his face, to make his presence known, but at least he felt the need, even if only out of obligation, to be there.

Helen wakes me up in the evening and tells me she has made supper if I'm hungry. I am. I don't even remember the last time I've eaten and, though I doubt I'll be able to stomach much, I drag myself up the stairs and to the kitchen table. Helen has made spaghetti and garlic bread, set out on the table in bowls rather than the pans they were cooked in like Mom would have done. I sit and eat and Helen sits and watches me without saying anything. Without trying to get me to talk. The image of Dad won't leave my mind. It plays over and over again like a haunting, and I wonder if it was really him.

When I open my mouth, my voice comes out little more than a whisper.

"Helen?"

"Yes, Jake?" She answers slowly and quietly, neither surprised nor delighted that I'm finally speaking.

"Do you think . . ." I start. "I mean, was my Dad there? At the funeral?"

"I don't know, Jake. But I'm sure he was."

"Because I saw him. I think I did. Up in the balcony. I couldn't really see his face, but it was him, I think."

"Have you ever been to a funeral before today, Jake?"

"I think so," I say. "Somebody from my grade at school died of cancer years ago. We were given the option to skip school to go to her funeral, so I went."

"The thing about funerals, Jake, that I'm not sure you understand, is that they don't just happen."

"I don't know what you mean."

"What I mean, Jake, is that when someone dies, their funeral doesn't just follow automatically. It has to be planned. Arrangements must be made, with the church, the funeral home, the flower shop. There's a lot of calling around and talking and planning that go into a funeral."

"Who . . ."

"I don't know, Jake. Not for sure. But it wasn't me. And it sure wasn't your mother."

That's when I know. Dad. He did it. He didn't come home—won't come home anymore now—but he did what needed to be done. It may have been a final act, a sort of kiss goodbye to me, to Mom, especially to Kyle, but he did it. He made the calls, picked out the casket, spent the money. He did what a father would do; he took care of his son, his obligations.

Grand County isn't a big place. A lot of people from Clouton come to Browerton to shop, get groceries, that kind of thing. I might see Dad again, might run into him somewhere. But even if I don't, the picture I have in my head of him standing in the balcony of Faith Lutheran Church on the day of his youngest son's funeral, leaning—defeated in some ways, I imagine, broken, but still there—is enough, I think. It's the Dad I want to remember, and I think it's the one I will.

After I finish eating, Helen puts the leftovers away and we sit at the table and talk for hours. I feel normal again, at least in some ways. I've slept a little, eaten a little. Some of my strength is back. Eventually, the conversation turns to Mom and I realize that I understand nothing about where she is and why. I know so little about her condition and how it's treated and what they do to her when she's taken away. Helen tells me a little—padded rooms, restraints, ugly stuff that I don't want to see—but that stuff is only for the first day or two, before they get her stabilized and back on her medicine. A visit to her now, Helen says, would likely be much like any hospital visit. I would find her in her own room, with a bed, a T.V. "Would you like to visit her, Jake?" Helen asks. "Is that something you'd like to do?"

Chapter 17

First thing in the morning, I'm up and in the shower—something else I haven't done in a few days—and surprised again by how much better I'm feeling. I stand and let the warm water beat down on my back and close my eyes, thinking of Jackie. I never even told her about Kyle's funeral, never told her that it was yesterday. Will she mind? Will she be mad that I didn't let her know? Is a funeral really something that you invite someone to? Does she even care about me enough to give a damn one way or the other? I have no way to get a hold of her now, but I imagine she'll show up when the time is right. She always does.

I put on the same clothes that I wore to Kyle's funeral, which I find hanging in my closet (courtesy of Helen—I had thrown them in a heap on my bedroom floor) and Helen and I leave the house by nine o' clock. The day is surprisingly cool, with the kind of air that smells clean, like rain. I roll down the passenger side window of Helen's car and the cool breeze ruffles my hair and it feels good. I see the world in color again—leaves, houses, cars, a girl with a big, floppy, yellow hat. Helen pulls up in front of the door of the Browerton hospital, leaves the car in gear.

"Aren't you coming in?" I ask her.

"I'm going to let you go alone, Jake," she tells me. "I think your mother will be happy to get some time with you."

I get out of the car and I'm mad at myself because I don't want to go in. I don't want to do it. Part of me wants to stand outside while Helen drives away, then just walk. Where, I don't know, but anywhere would be better than here. I shouldn't feel this way, I know. I should be excited to see my mother, concerned for her. And I suppose I am, but I also feel pressure that I can't quite describe, like something is expected of me and I don't know what it is. In a way, I feel like I'm on trial—like I'm going to some sort of interview rather than to visit my sick mother. I realize, suddenly and surely, that I'm nervous because I feel like I'm

99

about to meet someone for the first time, and I have to make a good impression. For god's sake, I dressed up like I'm going to church just to come to the hospital. I still don't know what to expect, but I'm here and I know I have to do it, so I go inside.

Two fat women that could be sisters sit at a desk just a few steps past the front door. One of them glances up at me, then licks her finger and goes back to shuffling through a pile of papers on the desk in front of her. I approach the desk with my hands in my pockets.

"Hi." My voice cracks.

"Hello," the other lady says. "What can I help you with today?"

"I'm here to see my . . . uh, I'm here to visit a patient."

"And which patient might that be, sir?"

"Patty Withers," I say. "Patricia. Patricia Withers."

She types my mother's name, lightning fast, into a computer. Frowns.

"I'll have to call you a security escort," she says, trying hard to smile at me. "If you'll have a seat right there," she points to a small waiting area, "I'll call your name when your escort arrives."

"Thanks," I say. Her eyebrows raise and she opens her mouth, but I beat her to the punch. "I'm Jacob Withers," I tell her. "Her son."

A few minutes later, the woman calls my name and an older man with a bad comb-over is standing at the desk, hands on hips. His back is bent, shoulders slumped forward. He carries a massive gut despite his thin arms and legs, and his face is pock-marked and droopy, his mouth an open gape, his earlobes oversized. If this guy is Browerton Hospital's finest, I can only assume that this place is a zoo. I really can't picture this guy striking enough fear into anyone to defuse a situation. Even his uniform is generic, black high-water slacks and a khaki colored polo shirt with a gold pin over the left side of the chest that reads "Alvin," and, under that, "security." He tells me to follow him, then lopes to an elevator just to the right of the desk. He doesn't look at me or speak as we wait for the elevator, and he remains silent as the doors open and we step in. He pushes the button for the third floor and the doors close. The elevator is painfully quiet, with no music of any kind, and I notice that Alvin is a mouth-breather. Every breath he takes protrudes his lips from his mouth, making a sound almost like he's snoring. When the doors open, we get off on the third floor, and Alvin walks to a nearby desk, then turns and looks at me like I'm supposed to know what to do.

"Hello, Alvin," says a lady seated at the desk. "Who's your friend?" Then, without giving Alvin a chance to answer, she addresses me: "Are you here to see someone, sir?"

"Ah, yeah," I stammer. "Patricia Withers."

She types a few things into the computer.

"Okay, and are you immediate family?"

"Yeah. I'm Jake. I'm her son."

She types again.

"Okay, Alvin," she says. "We can take it from here. Thanks for your help."

Alvin nods and mumbles, then heads back to the elevator and disappears inside.

"I hope he didn't scare you too much," she says, whispering with her hand shielding her mouth. "There's really no need for the whole security escort thing. He only got the job 'cause he's Dr. Bilton's cousin." I nod like I know who Dr. Bilton is. "Plus he's kind of 'special' if you know what I mean," she says, smiling. "Anyway, if you'll hang tight for just a second, I'll get someone to help you." She picks up the phone and tells someone on the other end who I am and why I'm here. Less than a minute later, a young male nurse opens a door next to the desk that leads into the ward.

"Hi, I'm Will," he says. He extends his hand and I shake it. "I'm your mother's nurse today. I'm not sure how she'll be right now. She's been pretty drowsy on account of her medication, but she should at least be responsive, albeit probably pretty tired." He stops and motions to a door. "She's right in here. Go ahead and buzz me if you need anything." Will walks down the hallway with a bounce in his step, and, looking around the ward, I realize it's nothing like I had imagined. I always thought places like this would be pretty much *One Flew Over the Cuckoo's Nest* come to life. You know—guys in white robes all over the place drooling and hitting their heads against the wall and pissing their pants and all that. But the place is actually not too bad. Pretty much just looks like any other hospital hallway—clean and sterile, surprisingly sane.

The inside of Mom's room is more of the same: white walls, white floor tiles, grey curtains. Mom is lying in bed with her eyes closed. Her hair looks damp and wispy, and somehow, lighter than before. Her skin is waxy and tight, her eyes sunken and rimmed by dark blotches. I sit in a chair beside her bed and wonder if I should bother her. Maybe I should just leave. I tried, right? I mean, when she gets out of here, at least I can tell her that I came to see her, even if she didn't know I was there. I stand and walk to the window on the other side of the bed. Pulling the curtain to the side, I see the surprisingly beautiful skyline of Browerton. Sure, it's not much—an old hotel, the high school, the water tower, but from this angle it's somehow new. From this angle, it's almost like seeing the town I've lived my whole life in for the first time. A dry, crackling voice behind me. Mom. I turn to her.

"What's that, Ma?"

"Water," she says, and her eyes are still closed.

I pick up a waxed paper cup from the bedside table and bring the straw to her lips. She drinks just a little, then waves the cup away.

"How do you feel, Ma? Can I get anything else for you?"

"I'm okay," she says. "Just tired." She opens her eyes and wriggles under the blankets.

"Are you comfortable? Wanna sit up or something?"

I grab under her arms and scoot her back in the bed, then readjust her pillows so she's sitting upright.

"That better?" I ask. She nods. "Been watching anything good on T.V.?" I pick up the remote from the bedside table and click the T.V. on.

"No," she says.

"Nothin' good on, huh?" I ask.

"No T.V." she says, reaching for the remote. I give it to her and she shuts the T.V. off. Sets the remote on the bed next to her, out of my reach.

We sit silent for a while, both looking out the window. Several times I almost speak, but I don't know what to say. I would only be speaking to break the silence, and I feel like this situation deserves more. Like I shouldn't speak unless what I say will actually matter, actually make a difference. I wish I could tell if Mom has gotten any better but I really can't. I'd like to get her to talk to me, but I don't know what to say. Do I ask about Kyle? About the funeral? Does she know yet? Does she get it?

"Has anyone else come to visit, Ma?" I ask. "Any of the neighbors?"

"Nope," she says. "Or if anyone has, I didn't see them. I've been very tired. Been sleeping a lot." She brings her right hand to her face, slowly and with some effort, and rubs at her eyes. "Kyle was here though. Just this morning." She says it like it's the most normal thing in the world—like it would be strange if he hadn't been here. "Only it wasn't really him, Jake. He could walk and he could talk, just the same as anyone." She turns her face to me. "Does that make sense, Jake? Could it? My little Kylie was here—I know it was him—but it was almost like the him that never was. Almost like the him that would have been if he . . ." She trails off and turns back to the window. "Do you think it was his ghost, Jake? Because I do. I was never really sure if I believed in ghosts before today, Jake, but I do now."

"Yeah, Ma," I tell her. "It does make sense, and I do believe it's possible. I do think he was here. He's probably still with us right now." I'm not really sure if I believe what I'm saying, or if I'm just trying to make her feel understood.

"No," she says, shaking her head. "No, he's gone. He came to say goodbye. Told me that he loved me but he had to go and that we would see each other again someday, but not soon. Not now."

"So, did you . . ." I begin, not sure what exactly I should say. This has to be a good sign. She did say she thinks it was a ghost. She doesn't think he's still alive. "I mean . . . his funeral was yesterday."

She looks at me again and nods, her eyes damp. "He told me that, too."

"Kyle told you?"

She nods again. "He said it was beautiful. He was very happy to see everyone there. He can fly now, you know. He can go anywhere and do anything and see anything he wants. He's free." She nods slowly, her eyes vacant. "He's finally, finally free."

I nod like I understand, but I can't help but wonder if this has done her any good—if her time here has made her any better, or if it ever will. She seems to know Kyle is dead, but she seems convinced that he's no less present because of it. Is that any better? Is *she* any better?

"And you know what part he liked best, Jake?"

I shake my head. "No, Ma," I say. "What?"

"Your playing," she says. "The wonderful song you played for him. He told me you played his favorite song, and you let him play too. He said he'll never forget it, that it's one of the best memories he's got to take with him."

My head spins and I wonder if it's possible. Someone must have been here, told her what happened at the funeral. One of the neighbors or somebody. But who?

"Who told you that, Ma?" I ask. "Who told you I played at the funeral?"

"Kyle told me, dear," she says. "I already told you."

"Be serious, Ma," I say. "Tell me who it was. Someone was here. Do you remember? Do you remember who told you?"

"No one has been here but Kyle, Jake," she says. "It's just like I told you. Kyle was here this morning, and no one was here before or since, until you walked in just now."

"That can't be," I say, shaking my head. But I'm not so sure. I felt like he was there with me when I played, I really did. I felt like he helped me, like he guided my hands. But the mind is powerful, I know that. I've always believed that people are haunted by the ghosts of their loved ones because they want so badly to believe they're not gone, that their minds make things up, create scenarios to help them deal with the loss. But if no one's been here to visit, how could Mom know?

"Someone must have been here, Ma," I say. "Maybe you were sort of sleeping or something but your mind remembers what they told you, or . . ."

She's not listening. She's turned to the window again, her eyes distant, unseeing.

"Tired," she says, her lips barely moving. I stand and help her to lie back down. She nestles into the blankets and sighs deeply, closes her eyes. I sit silently for several minutes until I hear her breathing slow down and grow heavy. The room is quiet and still and makes me calm and aware. I sit for awhile and just sort of look around the room, at the greyish machines blipping beside the bed, and the cream-colored wallpaper. Even after his death, my mother's mind is filled only with thoughts of Kyle. I'm sitting right here beside her and still, all she can talk about is him. She didn't ask how the funeral was or ask how I am. Ask me how things have been, how I'm taking it all. And yet I've never talked to her about how I feel about it. About her. About not really ever feeling like I had a mom to raise me, a mom who cared about me. Her attention was always on either Kyle or herself, while I was alone.

"I don't know if you can hear me or not, Ma," I begin. "Actually, I kind of hope you can't." I wait a few seconds, but she doesn't stir. She's beginning to snore. "I have some good memories—not very many, but some—from when I was little. Before Kyle was born, I mean. You used to play with me sometimes and talk to me and pay attention to me, but then after Kyle was born, you never did any of that anymore. It seems like the only times you interacted with anyone was when you were feeding Kyle, or playing with him, or putting him to bed, or whatever."

Outside, a small black and grey bird lands on a tree. Flits from branch to branch. Restless.

"And it's just that . . . Well, it might sound dumb, but I think it changed me—that you changed me. I mean, I think I could have been . . . different somehow. Happier or something, maybe, if you would have just been there for me more. Talked to me or just looked at me or paid some attention to me somehow. I know I never told you, and I never even really let on, but I always felt like something was wrong with me. Like I wasn't really part of the family or something. Like you didn't really want me to be."

The bird wisps into the air and lands on the windowsill outside, like it was carried by the wind.

"You know, 'cause really, Ma, what the hell have I done? In my life, I mean? What have I really done? Nothing. I have a crappy job and pretty much no friends and I pretty much just sit around at home. I guess what I mean is, maybe I feel like I could have done something. Maybe I feel like I could have something going for me if I just would have had some kind of a push. Some support of some kind from you. A reason to believe that I could do something, or that anything was even worth doing. A reason to believe that you care what happens to me."

I'm starting to cry now. I'm just talking in circles anyway, and she can't even hear me. Plus if I keep going I'm just going to get pissed or sad or something and end up making an ass of myself in front of a nurse or somebody. I wipe my face and I'm standing up to leave when she speaks.

"Sit down."

I sit.

"I'm tired, Jake," she says, "and I don't feel great, so listen up, 'cause I don't want to repeat myself." Her eyes are open and alert. She looks like a different person, like she's just snapped out of the last ten years of her life and become the woman I've dreamt about, the one my father fell in love with. "I know I've had my problems and I haven't been the best mother in the world. That's not news to anyone. And I'm not even going to go into my problems, because that's all old hat and it's not what this is about anyway." She scoots up in the bed on her own power, sits up, and turns to face me. I feel like I'm meeting my real mother for the first time. "I don't think you know what it was like for me when Kyle was born, Jake. Before Kyle came along I felt worthless. I felt about how you must feel right now, I guess. I knew what a mother was supposed to be and I knew I hadn't really been one. When Kyle was born, I felt like I finally had that chance. I could finally be someone's entire world. I could finally feel as important and loved and necessary as a mother should feel."

"What about me, Mom?" I ask. "Why couldn't you have been that Mother for *me*?"

Her eyes grow narrow, softer. Her shoulders slump.

"Because you didn't need me, Jake," she says. "You didn't need me. You're special, Jake. I suppose I haven't reminded you of that enough, but you are one of the most amazing people I've ever met. I'm as jealous of you as I am proud. I could tell from the moment I held you in my arms that you wouldn't need me. You've got something special, Jake. Something that no one else in this world has—at least not anyone I've met. For God's sake, Jake, the way you play piano. The way you were playing all that hoity-toity Bach and everything by the time you were—what?—three years old? Four? And the way you think. The things you see. The things you understand, about people, about the world."

I don't know what to say; I want her to just keep going.

"I know I was never really there for you, Jake, and it has bothered me. It still does. But Kyle was what I needed to feel whole and I knew that I would never be what you needed. The bottom line, Jake, is that I knew you'd be fine. I knew you could do it all on your own. Anything at all that you dreamed you could do, with or without me or anyone. I believed it then and I believe it now."

She scoots back into a prone position and closes her eyes. Neither of us say anything more. Within moments, she's asleep again.

I almost ask the woman at the desk if Mom had, in fact, had any other visitors, but instead I just walk right on past, straight to the elevators, because I believe her.

I believe her.

Chapter 18

Mom was only in the hospital for a few more days and now that she's home, it's been business as usual for the most part. I mean, she's definitely more aware—more present, or however you want to say it—but she spends a lot of time in her room just resting and sleeping because of the medications they have her on. I guess the doctor said she'll feel a little off for awhile, but then her body will adjust and she should be feeling better than she has in a long time.

It's officially fall now—most of the trees are bare, biting winds are already warning of winter, and school is back in session. Not that I've gone yet. I never had the best attendance in school anyway, but I do plan to go this year. I really do. It's just that I feel like Mom needs someone here for her right now and it might as well be me. I'm sure Helen would be happy to do it (what else does she have to do these days?), but I figure it's the least I can do. Even if she never really did take care of me, it's all good now. I get it.

I didn't see Jackie for a while after the whole incident at her house—maybe a week or so, almost two. I suppose she was pretty embarrassed about her situation. I mean, she did *lie* to me after all. There's no other way to put it. I haven't talked to her about that yet and, knowing me, I probably won't. But I will have a good chance to talk to her about that or anything else that comes up later tonight. See, she showed up at the store the other day while I was working (yup, I'm back at the grind), and we didn't get a chance to talk much, but I ended up asking her if she wanted to go to this school dance with me. Kind of weird, me asking a girl to a dance—especially considering that I've never been to one—but it just sort of came out of my mouth. My co-worker Geoff was asking me if I was going, and who I was going to take, and he wouldn't shut up about it and I guess it was on my mind, so I just sort of asked her, out of the blue, without really thinking about it. Maybe it's part of my upcoming campaign to be a real person: have a good relationship with

107

Erik P. Block

family, go to work regularly, attend school and school functions. Who knows. So anyway, she said 'yes,' and she's coming to pick me up at 7:00 tonight. Manly, I know.

It's sort of unlike me to get all worked up about stuff like this, but with it being my first real dance—hell, my first real *date*—I'm letting myself worry. I was really hoping that I wouldn't have to wear the khaki pants and black shirt combo that I've come to call "the funeral get-up," so I was digging through my closet to see if I could find anything else. You know—something a little dressy without being too uppity. Something I could look half decent in without feeling like I'm 60 years old. Anyway, I ended up digging through the cubby hole under the staircase and I found this awesome leisure suit. Straight up flappy collar, bell-bottom, John Travolta shit. Must have been Dad's from 20 years ago. I'm quite a bit taller than he is, so the pants come off a little bit high-waterish, but the whole thing's all right overall. I'll probably stand out a little bit at the dance (I don't even know if people dress up for these things), but hey—I gotta be me, right?

I start getting really nervous around 5:00, even though Jackie won't be here for another two hours. Normally I wasn't that nervous to spend time with her, but this is different. We'll be in public. Together. People will see us. Which is scary, but it's also very, very exciting. Jackie's got style. She's got class. She commands a room. And I'm going to be walking in with her.

I look in the mirror and decide that I need to take a shower and wash my hair and face, even though I already did before work this morning. After my shower, I dry off and even put a little gel in my hair. I put the suit on and take a look at myself in the full length mirror on the back of my bedroom door. I don't look too bad. In fact, I look pretty damn good. I'm ready to do this.

I'm sitting in the living room, looking out the picture window and fidgeting, when Jackie pulls into the driveway. I rush to the door trying to look relaxed, and open it before she even knocks.

She's wearing the yellow dress.

She looks nervous, her eyes flitting from her bright red high-heeled shoes, up to my face, and back again. She's smiling a nervous half-smile, tracing a figure over and over with her turned-in right foot.

"Hey," I say and stand aside to let her in the door.

"Hi," she says. "Nice suit." She doesn't move. We both just stand and sort of look at each other for a little while. She looks amazing, exactly as she looked the day we met, but somehow different, too. Somehow older, more real. She's holding a small handbag in front of her, her hands clenching and unclenching.

"Wanna come in for a minute or something?" I ask. "I should go say goodbye to my mom, anyway." She steps in the door and onto the landing. "Hey, do you want to meet her? I mean, you never really have. She's . . . better. I mean, she knows what's going on and she could talk to you and everything."

"We should just go," she says. "I don't want to be late." She steps back out onto the stoop. "Come on."

"Ah . . . okay." I start to step outside, then turn and call up the stairs, "Bye, Ma!"

On the drive to the school, Jackie reaches under her seat and pulls out a small bottle of booze and takes a drink. Besides the semi-formal wear, it's just like the night we went out to the field with the giant rock—only a few nights ago, but it feels like months. Years. She passes the bottle to me and I almost tip it back for my customary three-count, but I hand it back instead.

"Not drinkin' tonight?" she asks. "Gotta be up early to watch cartoons tomorrow or something, little man?"

"Nah," I chuckle. "I just . . . I don't know, I wanna be all here tonight. I wanna be present."

She shrugs and takes another drink. "Suit yourself, I guess. That might be better, actually. You know—in case I need a babysitter." She shoots me that killer smile.

"You look really nice, by the way," I say.

"Thanks," she says, "but you've already seen me in this dress, right?"

"Yeah. But it's a nice dress. You look good in it. It's how I picture you. I mean, when I call up a picture of you in my head, this is what I see. Exactly what's sitting next to me right now is what I see."

She glances at me quick and smiles, then takes a drink. Winces.

"And those shoes are something else," I say. "Like Dorothy or something."

"I was afraid you'd say that," she says. "It's not the first time I've heard it, I'll tell you that." She looks down at her shoes, taps her heels together twice, and giggles. "You look a lot better," she says. "I mean, your face has really healed up."

"Yeah," I say. "I still got a little ways to go, but thanks for noticing." I'm proud of how well I'm carrying on without having to be drunk. I haven't really spent much time around Jackie (or any girl) without the aid of my favorite social crutch, so this is sort of a test. So far I'm passing. "I hope they're not giving breathalyzers at the door."

"What?" Jackie asks. "Are you serious?"

"Yeah," I say. "I don't know if they've ever actually done it at my school—I mean, I've never actually been to a dance. But I've heard something about it on T.V., I think. That schools do that."

"That's fucked," she says. "That's exactly what I need."

"What are you worried about?" I ask. "What are they gonna do, kick you out of school? You graduated. And you didn't go to this school anyway."

"Yeah, but think about it," she says. "You know how schools can be about that shit. How everyone can be. Everybody's so damn scared that we're going to drink or smoke or have sex or whatever—that we're going to grow up—that they go around overreacting about everything. If I got caught drinking tonight, I'd lose my license. Hell, they'd probably find a way to take my car away from me or make me go *back* to school or something."

"Yeah," I say. "I guess."

When we pull into the school parking lot, it's still pretty empty. It's only a little after 7:00 and the dance doesn't actually start until 8:00. Jackie takes a spot in the back of the lot, far from the auditorium door.

"So," she says. "We're early."

"Yup."

"What should we do?"

"I don't know," I say. "I guess we just sit here until they open the doors."

She takes another pull from the bottle and lights a cigarette, which she holds out the open window with her left hand.

"Are you sure that's a good idea?" I say. "I mean, we are on school grounds. I don't mean to be a goody-goody or anything, but we don't have to flaunt it."

Jackie just grunts a little and takes a drag. Flicks her freshly-lit cigarette out the window.

"I'm bored," she says. "Let's go check it out."

"Check what out?"

"I don't know," she says. "The dance. The school. Let's go see what's going on." I start to tell her that we can't get in yet, but she's not listening. She's out of the car and heading across the parking lot before I get a chance to unbuckle my seatbelt.

I hurry to catch up with Jackie, and as I approach, she tosses her keys over her shoulder. I catch them.

"You should hang onto these," she says. "I'm gonna get wasted tonight."

"How?" I ask. "The booze is in the car." She turns, holds up her handbag, and says matter-of-factly, "flask."

To my surprise, the outer auditorium door is open, and a small line has gathered at the inner door where the art teacher, Mr. Fennek, is sitting at a table with some other guy I don't recognize, collecting money. No breathalyzers in sight. Instead of getting in line, Jackie just walks right on past like she's the only one in the hallway.

"There a bathroom down here?" She asks. "I gotta go."

"Yeah," I say. "I think so. Just down the hall here and to the right." I stop at the corner and park myself against the wall. "I'll wait for you here . . ." I start to say, but Jackie grabs my wrist and pulls me along down the hallway. And into the bathroom. Luckily, there's no one else inside.

"I . . . don't really know if I'm comfortable with this," I say. "I probably shouldn't be in here."

"Sure you should," she says. "Quit being a pussy."

"I'm not being a pussy. I just don't . . ."

Before I can finish, Jackie grabs me by both arms and pulls me to her, kissing me hard on the mouth. I'm thrilled and surprised and I don't really know what to do. I've never really done this type of thing with a girl before and I'm bothered by the fact that the only thought in my head is *I wonder if I'm doing this right*. She holds me tight to her with her lips pressed to mine for several seconds, then opens her eyes and nudges me backward.

"What?" she asks. "Something wrong?"

"No," I say. "No, not at all. I just . . . you just took me by surprise is all, and I didn't really . . . I mean . . . I just don't really . . . know what to do, I guess."

"Weird," is all she says before unzipping her handbag and taking out the flask.

"Uh . . ." I stammer, "we should be careful. What if a teacher comes in or something?"

"Here," she says, opening a stall door and stepping in. I step in behind her. She takes a drink from the flask and offers it to me. I wave it off. I want to talk to her about Dad, but I don't think this is the best time. If I was drunk, I'd have an easier time bringing it up, but knowing me, I'll never do it unless I do it now. Maybe this is my only chance.

"How long has he been with your mom?" I ask.

"What?" She knows what I'm talking about, but I've taken her by surprise. "Oh. I . . . Jake, do we have to? Can we talk about this some other time? I just want tonight to be fun. Just you and me, having fun. Can we do that? Just for tonight, please?"

"I don't know," I say. "I mean, I want tonight to be fun, too. This is great. I'm really happy; honestly, I am. But I need to know this. I think I need to know it now. How long?"

112 | Erik P. Block

She sighs loudly.

"Fine," she says. "I don't know how long exactly. A while. Quite a while."

"Quite a while?" I ask. "Can you do any better? A month? A year? Five years? What?"

"I don't know," she says again. "I guess, like . . ." she rolls her eyes upward, thinking, ". . . three years? Four? I swear to God, Jake, I'm really not sure."

I suddenly feel sick again, like I did when Dad stepped out of the bathroom. I feel like the world is rushing in on me, taking away my air and smothering me.

"No, wait," she says. "He was there for my surprise party when I turned thirteen. So five years at least. Five and a half."

"And how long did you know?" I ask. "I mean, how long did you know who he was? That he was my dad?"

"I swear to God, Jake, I had no idea," she pleads, touching my forearm gently. "I didn't know until that night at the bar, when Rosy said his name. I never even knew your last name, Jake. If I had, I'm sure I would've figured it out."

"So why, then?" I ask. I feel my heart speeding up, my skin getting hot.

"Why what?" she asks.

"Why me? Why did you come see me after work that day? Why do you keep showing up? What is it about me if you didn't know?"

"Fine," she says. "I'll quit. I'll just quit *showing up*, as you say. Would that help? Is that what you want?"

"No," I say. "God, no. Not at all. I just don't understand."

"What is there to understand, Jake?" she asks. "You were the cute gas station guy. That's all. I just wanted to meet you. You're shy and interesting and . . . different." She looks at the floor, then up and into my eyes. "You intrigued me. You still do." She kisses me again, and I let her. I still don't feel like I understand any more about my father or his connection to Jackie's mother. I don't feel like I understand much about anything, but I'm happy. In this moment, sober and fumbling in a stall of the girls' bathroom at my high school, kissing this amazing woman who, for some reason, finds me intriguing, I am happy for the first time that I can remember.

After a fairly lengthy (and equally clumsy, at least on my part) make-out session, Jackie finishes the last of the whiskey, and we emerge from the girls' bathroom just in time to see Mr. Fennek open the auditorium doors. Jackie, obviously drunk, is struggling to walk straight. Fennek tells

Just Jake | 113

me it's seven bucks for a couple and I dig a wrinkled ten out of my wallet. He hands me three back and we walk through the door, me dragging Jackie by the hand, trying to get her sitting down before she gets us in trouble.

"You were acting really drunk back there," I say. "Fennek might have noticed."

"Who cares?" Jackie squawks, leaning into me. "Fuck 'im. Let's forget it and have some fuckin' fun!"

"Let's go sit down for a minute," I say. "Over there." I take her hand and point to the bleachers at the back of the auditorium. I should be excited about this, elated really, to be holding Jackie's hand in front of the entire school. But it doesn't feel right. She's too drunk. It shouldn't be like this. I could be anyone to her right now. Anyone at all.

I get her to sit for only a few seconds before she's up again, pulling me by the hand toward the dance floor.

"Come on!" she yells. "Let's dance!"

"I don't know," I say. "I don't think I'm ready yet. Can we just sit for a minute?" She curls her lower lip and pouts. "Please?"

"Fine," she says, shoulders slumped. She sits. "I just want to . . . . I don't know, *do* something. This is s'posed to be a fun night and we're just *sitting* here."

"The night's just started," I say. "There isn't even anyone here yet. Don't worry; we'll have fun."

She turns sideways and lays down on the bleacher, her head in my lap. Normally this would be perfect, but she's just so drunk. She's going to get us in trouble.

"Jackie," I hiss. "Get up. Don't lay down; you're going to pass out or something."

"I am not going to *pass out*," she says. "God, Jake." She sits back up and scoots away from me. Turns a shoulder to me and crosses her arms. She's not exactly making this the night I hoped it would be, but I'm still happy to be here with her. I slide over to her and tentatively put my arm around her back. She leans into me and puts her head on my shoulder; she's probably already forgotten she was mad.

I watch as couples file in steadily. Within twenty minutes or so, the place is looking pretty full. Not too many people are dancing yet, but they're mingling and having a good time. I feel my body stiffen as Ashlee walks in with a waifish brunette on his arm. He actually bothered to change out of his work shirt and baseball cap for the dance, which I imagine his date appreciates, even is she is a vapid idiot. Instead, he's wearing a white polo shirt and his hair is slicked back. His shoes are gigantic and bright white, like old hip-hop shoes. Fucking tool. The sight of him literally makes me shudder. He has a date and so does Jackie, so hopefully he'll leave her alone.

"Hey, there's Ashlee!" Jackie shouts, springing to attention. "Hey! Hey, Ash!" She's bouncing in her seat and waving frantically.

"Shhh! Jackie, seriously, you're being too loud," I say.

"Whatever," she says. Ashlee doesn't seem to have noticed us, and I'm just fine with it staying that way.

"What's his deal, anyway?" I ask. "Is he your cousin or something? How do you know him?"

"No," she slurs. "He's not my *cousin*, stupid. He's my boyfriend. Or was. *Ex*-boyfriend, sorry. I dumped him." She giggles like a little girl. Leans into me and whispers into my ear, "Don't worry, Jake. He has a small penis." I feel my face grow hot and flushed. I don't know if that was supposed to make me feel better, but I could have lived the rest of my life without that topic coming up.

"How long ago?" I ask. "How long ago did you guys break up?"

"I don't know," she says. "Like, forever ago. Spring, I think. Maybe like April? May?"

"So you guys are still close then, or what?" I ask. "You still hang out a lot and everything?"

"No," she says. Even as drunk as she is, she's managed to pick up on my anger and get a hold of herself a little. "When we saw him the other night at the bar, that was the first time in forever. I don't even remember the last time before that."

"That's comforting," I sneer. "With the way you are tonight, I don't know if you not remembering convinces me of much. You gonna remember tonight? I kinda doubt it." I feel the anger welling up inside of me, and I hate myself for losing control, but it feels good. It feels right.

Jackie stands up, rigid and defensive. "What the fuck is that supposed to mean? Even if I was still friends with Ashlee, what business would that be of yours? I could hang out with my ex-boyfriend every day and you wouldn't have shit to say about it!"

We're making a scene now. People on the dance floor have stopped moving and are watching us. Before I know it, Mr. Fennek is right in front of me.

"Problem here, Mr. Withers?" he asks.

"No," I say. "We're fine." Fennek doesn't look convinced. "Come on, Jackie, let's go. Let's get some air outside or something." I hold out my hand, hoping like hell that she'll just let this whole thing drop, at least for now, and come outside with me. We don't need Fennek smelling the booze on her. Jackie takes my hand somewhat reluctantly, and we go.

Just Jake | 115

In the hallway outside the auditorium I tell Jackie that we should go for a walk and have a cigarette and calm down.

"Yeah," she says. "Alright. I gotta go to the bathroom first." She seems like she's sobered up some, snapped out of it.

"I'll wait for you," I say.

"No, that's okay," she says. "You go ahead. I gotta check my make-up and stuff. I'll meet you at the car in a little while. You got my keys, right?"

I pull them out of my pocket. "Got 'em."

"Okay, see you soon," she says. "And Jake?"

"Yeah?"

"I'm sorry."

"Me too."

And then, as she's walking away, again: "I'm sorry."

I sit down in the car and let out a deep breath. Maybe I should just drop this whole Ashlee thing. Jackie's probably right: it really is none of my business. But I've always been a jealous person, I guess. I'm possessive of people and things. I guess I just don't trust that people will stick around, that things that seem good will stay the way they are. And right now, Jackie is definitely a good thing. She's the best thing I've got. I mean, it's great that Mom is doing better, and I guess Dad's just gone, not that I'm not pretty used to that by now. And Kyle's gone, but I feel like he's okay. I feel like he's where he should be and, somehow, I feel like he's still here too. I lie back in the car seat and, honestly, I feel pretty good. Things are finally ending up the way they should. I'm willing to look past the little spat we just had. I mean, we made out in the bathroom. That's pretty awesome. That would make for a hell of a story if I had anyone to tell.

I put the key in the ignition and turn it back. Flip on the radio. Some crappy Pink Floyd song. I flip through the stations but I don't find anything too good. Mostly country. I lie back again and wait. *I'm happy to be here with Jackie, even if she is too drunk, but something still doesn't feel right. My chest feels tight. I feel too anxious. Things are coming together though, with me and Jackie, with my family. Story of my life I guess, but what I was looking for wasn't really what I needed. I didn't need to bring Dad home and recreate the family I remembered. I just needed to understand my place in the one I have. Even if it is just me and Mom now.*

Partway through the third shitty country song there's still no sign of Jackie. I give it a few more songs, and when she still hasn't shown up I decide to go look for her. I'm worried I'll find her on her knees puking her guts out or, worse yet, passed out in a stall.

I make my way down the hallway and Fennek opens his mouth like he's going to say something, but I just look at the floor and walk right on past. A small gaggle of girls is standing outside the bathroom, so I'm not so sure I should go in.

"Hey," I say, approaching them. "Is there anyone in there?"

"Why, you gotta piss?" asks a short brunette. "I know you gotta sit down and everything, but there's toilets in the boys' room too. We won't tell anyone."

Bitch.

"I'm looking for . . ." I'm not sure what to call her, ". . . my date."

They ignore my comment and continue whispering and giggling. God, I hate girls. Most girls.

"Look," I say, "could one of you go in there and check for me? She's blonde, wearing a yellow dress? I just want to make sure she's okay."

"Fine," the little brunette says, rolling her eyes. "Whatever." She looks at her friends and shakes her head, then goes into the bathroom. Comes out again just a few seconds later. "She wearing bright red shoes?"

"Yeah."

"She's in there, alright." She sort of half-smiles and sucks air through her teeth.

"And?" I ask. "Is she okay?"

"I'll let you figure that out," she says, and blends back into the pile of skirts and poofy hair.

I open the door slowly, tentatively. "Jackie?" A rustling sound in the end stall. A muffled grunt. She's puking? Perfect. Exactly what I need. I gotta get her out of here before I get suspended or something. I actually plan to *be* a student this year. I peek under all the stall doors as I make my way through the bathroom, just to be sure there aren't any other ladies in here. Looks clear.

Sure enough, Jackie's bright red shoes are clearly visible below the door of the last stall. But there's another pair of shoes, too.

Big, bright white shoes.

"Jackie!" My heart is speeding up, my mind clouding over. I try to breathe deep, but I'm fucking losing it. "Jackie, what the fuck?"

"I'm fine," she says. "Just meet me outside, okay? I'll be there in a minute."

I grab the door handle and pull, but of course it's locked. I shake the door and yank back on it, over and over, as hard as I can. It swings open in my hand. Ashlee is sitting on the toilet lid and Jackie is straddled over him, her dress hiked up to reveal yellow panties. The dress straps are pulled down. For some reason, my eyes focus on the bra tan across her bare back. I don't look at her face, or his. She's talking, pleading I guess—I hope—but I don't really hear her. A rhythmic whooshing sound begins deep in my head and drowns out everything around me. *Vooo-vooo-vooo*, like some sick heartbeat. The world sort of goes grey, like at Kyle's funeral, only not the same. Not really the same at all.

My mouth opens and the words "I love you" come out. They hang in the air like a thick bubble, and I hate myself. I hate myself for saying it, and I hate myself for meaning it, and I hate myself for letting it happen. I'm through the hallway and in the parking lot within seconds, and I'm not even making my choices anymore. They're being made for me.

Jackie's car fires right up on the first try and I rev the engine, hard and loud. Throw it into gear and pull out of the parking lot, gravel flying. I pull the whiskey bottle out and empty what's left in one long pull. It hits me almost immediately. The warmth spreads and my head is swimming. I'd probably pray to God right now if I thought he existed. Don't know what I'd say exactly, but it would be nice to know someone was listening.

I speed through downtown and turn onto Swinden Strip. The booze settles in, takes full hold of me. I almost feel out of my body. Again, I'm struck by the realization that I'm not making decisions. I'm being pulled, manipulated. I'm talking to myself, some kind of gibberish mantra, over and over again, to the rhythm of the sickening heartbeat in my ears. The Strip is curvy as hell; I normally take this road pretty slow and careful, but my foot is heavy now, and I don't care. The yellow line is a thick blur with fuzzy edges; I can barely tell where the edge of the road ends and the steep bank leading down to the lake begins.

I come around a tight corner, and the road opens up into a long straightaway for as far as I can see, as far as my headlights will show me. I reach into my pocket, feeling for Kyle's picture, but it's not there. It hasn't been there for weeks. Images of Kyle, of Mom, of Dad, rush at me like road signs. Then an image of Jackie, but I push it away.

I stomp the gas pedal all the way to the floor, and the grey darkens to black. Crowds in on my vision from all sides. The inkblack night swallows me and I'm drifting, floating. I'm back at Kyle's funeral, sitting at the organ, playing for him. With him. The air softens. An image of Kyle, bright and smiling, glowing in rich color, settles in my mind, and I feel his hands take mine.

CPSIA information can be obtained at www.ICGtesting.com
Printed in the USA
267522BV00001B/69/P